Macaroni Boy

Also by Katherine Ayres

FAMILY TREE
NORTH BY NIGHT
SILVER DOLLAR GIRL
STEALING SOUTH

Katherine Ayres

Macaroni Boy

Delacorte Press

Published by
Delacorte Press
an imprint of
Random House Children's Books
a division of Random House, Inc.
1540 Broadway
New York, New York 10036

Visit us on the Web! www.randomhouse.com/kids
Educators and librarians, for a variety of teaching tools, visit us at
www.randomhouse.com/teachers

Library of Congress Cataloging-in-Publication Data
Ayres, Katherine.
Macaroni boy / Katherine Ayres.
p. cm.
Summary: In Pittsburgh in 1933, sixth-grader Mike Costa notices a
connection between several strange occurrences, but the only way he
can find out the truth about what's happening is to be nice to the class
bully. Includes historical facts.
ISBN 0-385-73016-0 (trade)—ISBN 0-385-90085-6 (lib. bdg.)
[1. Catholic schools—Fiction. 2. Schools—Fiction. 3. Family life—
Pennsylvania—Fiction. 4. Depressions—1929—Fiction. 5. Food
poisoning—Fiction. 6. Pittsburgh (Pa.)—History—20th century—Fiction.]
I. Title.
PZ7.A969 Mac 2003
[Fic]—dc21
2002006768

The text of this book is set in 12-point Garamond BE.

Book design by Angela Carlino
Printed in the United States of America
February 2003
10 9 8 7 6 5 4 3 2 1
BVG

This book is dedicated to
Diana Capriotti, who sparked the idea,
and to the Newell family—Carolyn, Jim, Jason
and Josh, who showed me its heart.

1

Macaroni Boy

"Hey! You! Macaroni Boy!"

Mike Costa whirled. He'd recognize that voice anywhere—Andy Simms, the worst kid in the Strip. *And I have the rotten luck to have him sitting right next to me in Sister Mary John's sixth-grade class.*

As Mike searched the sidewalk and alley behind him, his fingers curled into fists. With weasel-faced Simms on the loose, a guy needed to be ready.

"Macaroni Boy!" The shout came again, louder and closer this time. "I got a present for you."

A small, round blur flew in Mike's direction. He jumped backward, but not in time. Something smacked hard against his legs, spattering as it landed. *Cripes, a rotten apple.* Before he could take a breath, two more apples hit, mashing brown goo onto his socks and shoes.

"I'll get you for this," Mike shouted, running in the direction the apples had come from.

"Got to catch me first!"

Mike's shoes slapped against the pavement and he rounded the corner by a fruit market. As he raced onto the side street, he caught a glimpse of Simms, half a block ahead, ducking into an alleyway. Shoving past empty vegetable crates, Mike pushed his legs harder and turned into the alley, closing the distance between them.

In the narrow brick confines of the alley, Simms was a moving shadow, but Mike was sturdy and fast. He reached out to grab at Simms' skinny shoulder. "Got you, you punk."

"Says you, Macaroni Boy." Simms twisted away.

Mike ran and reached again, this time catching a good grip on the sleeve of Simms' coat. "You're a louse, Simms," he growled. Pulling closer, he aimed his fist at the kid's jaw and let it fly.

Simms ducked and the blow connected solidly with the side of his head. He grunted, then spun around and shoved, driving Mike belly-first into the railing of a fire escape. Simms yanked hard, freeing his arm.

For a moment Mike couldn't move, couldn't even breathe, his chest hurt so bad. By the time he could stand up and look around, all he could see was a brick wall. He ran his fingers along his ribs—sore, but nothing felt broken. His lungs burned as he tried to catch his breath, but each time he breathed in, a rotting, apple-y smell hit him smack in the nose.

He kicked at an empty tin can and sent it spinning up the alley, wishing he could kick Simms like that and send the bum into the cold, filthy water of the Allegheny River.

Mom would get after him for this, Mike knew. She had enough to do, keeping up with all the ordinary washing and ironing, she didn't need extra. He dragged himself from the alley and checked his legs to see how bad the damage was. His knickers seemed clean enough, but reddish-brown apple slime covered his socks and shoes.

Mike sped along Penn Avenue, past small shops and big food warehouses. He didn't stop until he reached 29th Street and his house. Ducking into the backyard, he peeled off his socks and shoes first. *Cripes, even my legs are covered,* he thought. *If Mom sees this I'll be in for it. Maybe I can clean up quick and nobody will know.*

Careful as a cat burglar, he eased open the back door and peered into the kitchen. Nobody. He inched inside and headed for the cellar stairs. Once in the cellar, he grabbed a tin pail and set it under the hot water tap. While the pail filled, he collected old rags and the bar of strong soap Mom used for washing clothes.

Phew. Even the cellar was starting to smell like

rotten apples. Mike turned off the water, grabbed the bucket and his supplies and ran back upstairs and outside. The cold stone of the back step chilled his feet, but he didn't let that stop him, just sat down to scrub the mess off. Once his legs looked clean, Mike dried them on an old ripped towel, then dumped the stained socks into the pail, swishing them around to loosen the worst of the muck.

"Hey there, Michael."

Mike looked up to see Grandpap marching across the backyard toward him with his fishing pole over one shoulder. A couple of ugly mud-brown river catfish dangled from a string in his hand. Mike wondered what sort of mood the old man would be in today.

"What you doing, kid?" Grandpap asked, stopping near the step. "And what's that smell? You smell like a cider press."

Good, Mike thought. *Grandpap's making sense. It must be one of his good days.* "A kid I know, he threw apples at me."

"Got you in the legs, did he? Must have pretty good aim. You get him back?"

"I chased him and I caught him too . . . ," Mike began.

"You scrubbing those socks to help your mother out? Or to keep from getting in trouble?" Grandpap's dark eyes gleamed.

"Both, I guess."

The old man chuckled. "Smart boy. *You* didn't throw

apples, did you? Hard times like we're having, it's a sin to waste good food. Lots of folks are going without."

That wasn't news. It was 1933 and the whole country was suffering from what the newspapers were calling *the Great Depression*. From New York to California, men were out of work and their families were going hungry. It was a tough time to be in the food business, Mike knew. The family business, Costa Brothers Fine Foods, hadn't folded yet but it sure wasn't raking in mountains of moolah these days.

"Well?" Grandpap asked. "Did you throw apples or not?"

Mike shook his head. "No, sir. I know better than to waste food. I just popped him one with my fist." He went back to soaping his socks.

"Good for you, Michael." Grandpap set down his fishing pole and reached into his pocket for the knife he used to clean fish. "Scrub your shoes off too," he said. "So you won't muck up your mother's clean floors."

"Yes, sir." *I'd like to mop the floors with Andy Simms,* Mike thought. *I'd mop so hard, Mom's floors would shine for a month. And good old Simms, he'd be waterlogged.*

". . . Well, boy, what do you say?"

Darn it. Grandpap was looking at Mike as if he expected an answer to a question. Mike hadn't been paying attention, so he didn't know whether he'd missed the question or Grandpap was having one of his forgetful spells.

"What do I say about what?" He shoved his dark hair back from his face.

"My fish, of course. Caught a couple nice ones. Plenty to share. Shall I have your mother fry up some for you?"

He really didn't need this, not on top of Simms. Mike looked down at the pile of fish guts at Grandpap's feet and tried to decide whether Grandpap was joking or the old man really didn't remember that Mike hated fish, especially those nasty-looking, long-whiskered river cats.

A laugh from Grandpap, then a sharp elbow in the ribs told Mike that Grandpap was joking. Okay, this really was a good day.

Mike wrinkled up his nose. "No thanks, Grandpap. You can keep your ugly catfish. I don't eat anything with whiskers. Besides, those fish stink worse than my socks and shoes." He picked up the left shoe and swiped at it with his soapy rag.

Grandpap laughed again. "Tell you what, once you wash off all the mess, dab a little kerosene onto a rag and mix it with shoe polish. That will kill off the smell and your shoes will look as good as new. Nobody will suspect a thing." The old man winked. "Tough guys like us, we gotta stick together."

Mike grinned and winked back. "Thanks."

"You're welcome. And when you get a chance, get rid of this garbage for me, will you?" Grandpap stood and pointed toward the fish heads at his feet.

"Yes, sir." Mike would have to hold his breath to clean up the fish mess, but it was worth it for Grandpap to be in such a good mood. He was like his old self, teasing and joking, Mike realized. That had to be a good sign.

Grandpap carried his cleaned fish into the kitchen as Mike finished wiping off his shoes.

Holding his breath, Mike shoveled Grandpap's mess onto a thick newspaper and studied the bloody fish heads and guts. *Nasty,* he thought. *How could anybody eat fish, especially after cleaning them?*

He was bending to fold the newspapers into a tight bundle when an idea crept into his mind, sneaky as a rat. Those fish guts kinda looked like a present, wrapped up nice in newspaper. And by tomorrow they'd be plenty ripe. They'd smell ten times worse than rotten apples.

Do I dare? Sure, I'll do it, he decided, tucking the package between a rock and the back fence. *Happy birthday to you, Andy Simms.*

2

Out the Window

That night as Mike lay in bed, his ribs ached where he'd banged into that darned fire escape. He rolled from his side to his back so it wouldn't hurt so much and closed his eyes, ready for sleep. He took a deep breath, and then another, but before even the first wave of drowsiness could hit, a loud commotion sounded from behind the house.

Mike sat up in bed and listened. A yowling, screeching noise rose from the backyard. Bolting from the bed, he ran to the back window, pressed his face against the glass and looked out.

From his attic window, he could see motion near

the back fence, but it was too shadowy for him to recognize the animals making the noise. Cats probably, judging from the racket, and unless he missed his guess, they were fighting over his packet of fish guts. So much for that good idea.

Somebody opened a door, shouted at the cats and flung a rock in the direction of the fence; Mike heard it thud against the wood. Uncle Frank from next door, probably, since it didn't sound like it had come from Mike's house, and Uncle Frank did have a temper.

The cats quieted down, but Mike could still see them moving about in the dim light. *Bedtime snack,* he figured. *Hope they enjoy it.*

Mike had no appetite for fish guts, but he sure wouldn't have minded being outside. As he peered out the window, he could see past the back fence to the tracks and the produce yards, lit by streetlights. Beyond those flowed the Allegheny River, rippling black in the darkness.

It seemed like the whole city of Pittsburgh was awake that night—hundreds of men bustled about like ants. This one pushed a dolly through the crowded streets, that one heaved crates off the freight car, two more stood on the corner, and smoke plumes from their cigarettes rose in the glare of the streetlights. Wheels groaned, train engines huffed, and the men's voices filled the night, not with individual words, but with a deep-voiced hum that went on and on.

Even though he couldn't hear it clearly through the

window glass, Mike knew the sound—it was like a lullaby for him, he'd known it forever. As a little boy, he'd had nights when he woke up scared and couldn't get back to sleep. Grandpap had taken him outside on those nights and carried him around on his hip.

"Kid's bored sitting alone in his room," Grandpap would say. "I'll take him to the street for a little excitement and we'll tire him out." So out they would go, into the noise and bustle where men would call to Grandpap and toss him an apple or an orange for Mike to suck on.

Mike wondered now if maybe Grandpap had been bored too, sitting indoors after all the years he'd spent working nights. He'd gotten his start right down there, in the Strip, the narrow grid of streets, alleys and railroad tracks that filled the flats on the south bank of the Allegheny just upstream from the tall buildings of downtown Pittsburgh.

It was the warehouse district; they fed the whole city from the Strip, and Mike's family was a part of it. Grandpap and his brothers had come from Italy to this part of Pittsburgh years ago. They'd worked hard, saved their pennies and finally been able to start a business, Costa Brothers.

Mike traced his finger along the cold window glass and wished he could turn back the clock. The young, strong man who had hauled crates and started a business with his brothers, that Grandpap was long gone. So was the sturdy, comforting big guy who had carried a small boy about among oceans of apples and bananas, tomatoes and watermelons.

A worn, confused old man had taken his place. Mike sighed and studied the street below, as if somehow, by watching a man shove a heavy carton onto a wagon, he might catch a glimpse of Grandpap as he used to be. But all he saw was a bustling street, a long freight train and a wisp of pale smoke from a mill chimney upstream.

From the shadows, up near the train's engine, Mike heard a sudden clatter and saw men scrambling for something. He squinted and as his eyes adjusted to the distance he made out the shape of a coal car near the front of the train.

He'd heard rumors of such things; he just hadn't seen them with his own eyes before. Somebody on the train had *accidentally* spilled some coal, and men were picking up pieces and stuffing them into their coats, insurance against a cold winter's night and empty pockets. Boy, times were hard if grown men needed to elbow each other for small chunks of coal. They hadn't done that in the old days, when he was small, and the boxcars hadn't carried hobos either, those men who rode the rails in search of jobs. The country had been rich back then.

Still, Mike itched to be down on the street, among the men, part of the night. He'd like to find a small hunk of coal, not to burn but to keep, just to prove he'd seen the trainman spill it.

But he knew Pop would give him what for if he caught Mike sneaking out. So he watched awhile longer, then climbed back into bed, wrestling with his covers and wishing Grandpap could somehow get well.

As he lay there, his ribs started aching again, bringing the weasel face of Andy Simms into his mind. Maybe this was a night for wishing, Mike thought, for if one of those genie guys popped out of a bottle and offered him three wishes, Mike would sure know what to do with them. After bringing Grandpap back to his regular self, he'd somehow get Simms off his back.

Mike tried to remember when Simms had first started bothering him. It had crept up, a little at a time, like Grandpap's sickness, and just like Grandpap's sickness, there seemed no good reason for it.

When they'd first started school, Mike had barely noticed Simms. He was just there, sort of skinny and pasty-faced, the kind of guy who was always wiping his nose on his shirtsleeve. Mike had had plenty to do, learning to sit still and behave at the dry, dusty school desk while the nuns snapped out numbers and letters at him so fast it was hard for him to breathe. Besides, there were better guys to make friends with than a nose wiper, so Mike had mostly ignored Simms.

It wasn't until later, fourth grade or maybe fifth, that Simms started getting on his nerves. Mike had caught the rat on the playground grinding dirt into the mouth of a younger kid and had popped Simms one in the nose. Started a nosebleed too, Mike remembered, and well deserved.

Not that little kids weren't a pain sometimes, and if they pestered you enough, you maybe had to give them a quick cuff on the shoulder to show them who was boss. But just plain bullying for the fun of it, that turned Mike's stomach. Simms turned his stomach.

Gently, he ran his fingers along his left ribs. If he rolled carefully, he might be able to sleep on his right side instead of lying awake on his back all night. And to fall asleep, he needed something to think about, something good for a change, to take his mind off that lousy Simms.

The third wish from that genie, that would do it. Mike smiled as he imagined it. Some guys might wish for a real castle with knights and towers and moats. Others would pick a million dollars, cold cash, to spend however they wanted. Mike's wish would be cold too, but better than cash, and something he could never use up. He'd make that genie haul up an endless supply of chocolate ice cream. And a really big spoon.

3

The Carcass

When he woke the next morning, Mike discovered a line of small blue bruises along his left ribs. He punched his pillow. That Simms had left marks on him! At least they'd be under his clothes where they wouldn't show.

After breakfast he stepped into the backyard with a sturdy paper sack in his hand. Back by the fence he found shreds of newspaper, bloody and stained, all that was left of his neatly wrapped packet. Just as he'd figured, those cats had beaten him to Simms' present. Maybe that was for the best, he thought, shoving the sack into his pocket. Fish guts might have gotten him into trouble at school.

A few minutes later, with schoolbooks jammed in his satchel, he tagged along behind Pop and Uncle Frank as a chilly morning mist rolled off the river. In the pale, early light the Strip hummed. Down on Smallman Street the last of the boxcars were still lined up, and men, including Mike's youngest uncles, Tony and Roberto, were shoving carts and dollies loaded with crates of fresh food across the bumpy brick streets.

"Hey, Vince! Hey, Franco!" Men waved and called to Pop and Uncle Frank.

"Morning, boys, morning!" Pop called back. The loud voices filled the Strip with rough music as the men finished their long night's work. Mike grinned at the familiar sounds.

At the door to Costa Brothers Fine Foods, 2201 Penn Avenue, Pop reached into his pocket and pulled out the large iron key. With his usual flourish, he sailed the key into the lock and proclaimed, "Another day, another dollar. Come on, fellas, let's get to work." After opening the door, Pop and Uncle Frank strode to the loading dock in the back.

Mike grinned again, wondering if the door would even open without Pop's morning words to grease the lock. He stood for a moment as he usually did, listening to the thumps of crates and boxes being unloaded on the dock, and breathing in the warm, spicy scents. Overhead, six kinds of sausages hung from hooks in the ceiling timbers—everything from thin little pepperonis to nice big salamis. Beyond the sausages, he could see cheeses of all shapes and sizes aging in the air. Even though times were tough, their warehouse shelves bulged with sacks of macaroni, bunches of dried herbs, mounds of garlic and cans of tomatoes and tomato paste, small, medium and enormous. Big barrels stored olives, ripe and pungent in brine, while tins of olive oil lined another set of shelves. Yes, sir, depression or not, the Costa family wouldn't starve.

Time to get to work, Mike reminded himself. He set down his schoolbooks and opened the icebox that held the slicing cheeses. He pulled out a hunk of dry cheese rind, which he stuffed into his jacket pocket. Then he flipped on the lights for the cellar and carefully made his way down the brick stairs. Armed with a dented tin pail and with thick leather gloves to protect his fingers, he checked the large rattraps, one in each corner of the cellar. Empty. How could that be?

He checked the two traps under the stairs by the furnace, and two more along the back wall under the loading dock, where another set of wide stairs connected the cellar with the dock. More empties. What was going on?

The last trap he checked was full, and Mike dropped it into his pail. *Blast it,* he thought, *only one dumb rat in the whole cellar.* Usually he caught four or five and earned a penny apiece.

Pop would be disappointed. Unless Mike caught a few rats every day, the lousy critters would sneak upstairs and gnaw holes in sacks and boxes, stealing some food and spoiling the rest with their filth. Some merchants in the Strip used cats to protect their warehouses, but Pop thought traps were more reliable. Except that today their traps were mostly empty, so Mike's pockets would stay empty too. No ice cream.

Mike headed for the old stone slab and squatted. He dumped the trap, rat and all, onto the slab and reached for the heavy knife that lay on a rough wooden shelf above.

He was glad of the thick gloves. Dead or not, the rats were nasty. Even if they'd only been dead for a short while, they gave off a strong, foul smell. Mondays were the worst, Mike knew, for some of the Monday rats had been caught on Saturday night and had had a day and a half to work up a stink.

Carefully, he freed the dead rat from the spring-loaded bar that had snapped its neck; then he hacked off a good six inches of its tail. Mike tossed the rat back into the pail and set the thick, wiry tail in a wooden cigar box for Pop to check.

Now for the tricky part. He pulled the cheese rind from his pocket, broke off a hunk and placed it right where a hungry rat would reach for it. Then he stretched the spring and held the bar in place over the cheese while he secured the catch.

His uncle Tony had busted two fingers doing this part, which was why Mike had inherited the job, so he was plenty careful when he reset these big traps. They were strong enough to break a tough rat's neck, and he didn't want to put his fingers in danger.

After replacing the baited trap, he climbed the back steps and shoved open the sliding metal door to the loading dock, ready to dump the carcass into the brick-lined pit Pop had dug out by the alley. He bent to lift the heavy metal top, and as he did, the fumes stung his eyes. The quicklime they used took care of the dead rats in no time, but it gave off a strong chemical smell. A guy needed to hold his breath for this part of the job, and blink.

He was about to toss in the rat when an idea banged up against him and he dropped the lid back down. If not fish guts for Simms, then how about a dead rat? Nah, he'd get in even worse trouble for that with the Sisters. But only if he got caught. He did have a paper sack in his pocket. He could save the rat for after school and if he had a chance . . . well, he could decide about that after school.

Once he'd stowed the dead carcass in his paper sack, Mike returned to the store, took off his gloves and stashed them and the pail behind the cellar door. "Only one today, Pop," he announced, opening the cigar box with the single tail in it.

"You use enough cheese in the traps?"

"Yes, sir."

"Then maybe they're visiting our friend Vito at the fish market this week instead of us," Pop replied with a grin. "The rat you caught, though, on my good cheese, he died happy." He reached into his pocket and flipped a penny into the air in Mike's direction. "You work hard for the Sisters in school, now. Make the family proud."

Mike caught the coin and dropped it into his pocket, then reached for his books. "Yes, sir. I will, sir."

Frowning, Mike pushed open the door and stepped out onto the sidewalk. Although it wasn't his favorite part of the day, he didn't really hate his job with the traps. He was helping the family—part of the business— and in hard times like this, everybody needed to pitch in.

Besides, he was tough, he could handle it, and the work put good money in his pockets, usually five or six cents a day, plenty for ice cream. But now everything was going wrong, from the missing fish guts to the mostly empty traps. If he got even with Simms, maybe his luck would turn. Mike hoped so as he headed up Penn Avenue with the sturdy sack swinging in one hand.

4

Rat Boy

Shivering in the morning air, Mike wove along the busy sidewalks, where shopkeepers were out sweeping away the night's debris, and strong men loaded boxes and crates full of food onto trucks and horse-drawn carts. At 19th Street, he stopped and waited. Sure enough, his buddy Joseph Ryan was scrambling up the alley past the newsstand, his schoolbooks in one hand.

When he caught sight of Mike, he waved. "Sorry I'm late. My sisters hogged the bathroom all morning." He ran his fingers through his pale reddish hair, which looked like it hadn't seen a comb in a week. "You catch anything today?"

Mike clenched the top of the sack in his fingers and thought about telling Joseph his plans. It wouldn't hurt to have reinforcements, but if something went wrong, he didn't want Joseph to get in trouble. He decided to keep his plans to himself, at least for a while. "I caught one puny rat, and I got a penny left from yesterday," he said. "That makes all of two cents in my pocket. How about you?"

"I'm on easy street," Joseph replied. "Pop needed me to polish his shoes and shine up the brass on his uniform. Then Mom sent me to the store and said I could keep some of the change. Between us we've got enough for two cones. What will it be? Chocolate or strawberry?"

"I don't know," Mike answered, grinning. "Maybe a scoop of each. We've got all day to decide."

He and Joseph often pooled their cash. Some days when Mike caught a lot of rats, Joseph's cash supply was lean. Other days, like today, when Mike's pockets were nearly empty, Joseph was flush, so it worked out. Mr. Ryan was a cop, so he got paid regularly. Joseph's two older brothers worked in the Strip, like Mike's family did, so neither of their families would go hungry. Not like some.

He looked away as a dirty man with rough gray whiskers dug into a pile of rotting cabbages outside a small fruit and vegetable market. Mike shuddered. He couldn't help it; he always had creepy thoughts when they neared 17th Street, which led to St. Patrick's Church.

Father Cox, the priest there, had organized a soup kitchen and had even let the tramps and hobos set up a shantytown, right on Liberty Avenue on church land. Pop and most of the other merchants in the Strip pitched in and gave Father Cox free food when they could, but still the hobos searched the streets to fill their lean bellies.

As the boys reached the churchyard, Mike saw that a lot of the hobos were already up and stirring. Some men stood in line for breakfast, others tried to shave out of old dented tin pots. Mike looked away again and tried to think about how smooth that ice cream cone would taste on the way home from school. But he couldn't help shoving his hand into his pocket and holding his measly two pennies tight so they wouldn't jingle in front of the men.

Both boys sped up until the churchyard was out of sight. By the time they reached the gate of St. Patrick's School, a crowd had arrived and guys were playing stickball with a chewed-looking rubber ball and a slat from a fruit crate.

Mike and Joseph set their gear on the school steps and joined in, or tried to, but Andy Simms called out in a loud voice, "If it isn't Macaroni Boy! What did you eat today, spaghetti or them curled-up noodles that look like worms?"

Mike stepped away from Simms and toward the guys closest to the ball. "You're the worm, Simms," he called over his shoulder.

Simms didn't let up. "Hey, Joe Ryan. How come you hang around with this wop kid? If you don't watch out, he'll turn you into a spaghetti eater."

Mike tried to look bored by Simms' loud insults. Sure, some folks stuck with their own kind, especially the old folks, but most of the kids at St. Patrick's School got along okay whether they were Irish or Polish, Italian or Slovak. Shoot, everybody in Pop's big Italian family was nice to Mom, Irish or not. At least nowadays they were. Even Grandpap. And once Mike had been born, the Irish uncles had finally stopped fighting with the Italian ones.

"Aw, stow it, Simms," Joseph said. "He's half Irish anyway."

"Half Irish don't count," Simms replied. "And you know what else?" He turned and spoke even more loudly, so not a single guy in the schoolyard could help hearing. "I got old Macaroni Boy yesterday, got him good. I threw some rotten apples his way and he got so scared he nearly wet his pants." He let out a loud laugh and it echoed off the brick walls, as if the sound were being passed around the whole circle of guys.

Mike's belly and cheeks caught fire. He couldn't ignore the punk a minute longer. "Takes more than a couple rotten apples to scare me."

"Oh yeah? Prove it!"

Mike had planned to wait until after school, but what for? He glanced around. He didn't see any black-robed nuns nearby, so he bent and retrieved his paper sack. "Here you go, Simms," he shouted, tossing it right in his face. "Brought you a little dessert for your lunch."

Simms caught the sack and shook it, letting the rat fall to the ground. Murmurs arose from the crowd of boys, and a few grinned at Mike. It felt great. Joseph nudged him in the ribs and nodded toward the school doors.

That made sense to Mike. He'd won; no point hanging around. He'd taken half a dozen steps toward the doorway when Simms' voice caught up with him.

"Hey, Costa, is this what you crazy I-talians call lunch? Irish like us, we got better taste."

Mike turned, wishing he had another sack and another rat carcass to fling in Simms' face.

"Well, fellas," Simms went on in his loud, rude voice. "If old Costa likes rats for lunch, maybe he ain't going to be Macaroni Boy anymore. No, sir, maybe he just earned himself a new name."

Simms swaggered and grinned. "How about that, Rat Boy? You're moving up in the world."

5

Klavon's

"I should have waited," Mike groused as he and Joseph walked along Penn Avenue toward Klavon's after school. "I'm just lucky one of the Sisters didn't catch me."

"Speaking of Sisters, I tossed your rat into a trash can across the street from school this morning before the bell rang. Didn't want one of the teachers to find it. You'd have been in big trouble then."

"Thanks, Joseph."

"So tell me, what was that all about anyway?" Joseph asked. "Why'd you give Simms a dead rat?"

Mike explained.

"That's lousy," Joseph said.

Mike nodded. "*He's* lousy. He's so lousy, even his mother can't stand the sight of him."

Joseph laughed and Mike joined in. "It was bad today. Him and all his friends calling you Rat Boy. But you were tough, you didn't let it get you down."

Right, Mike thought, but his ears felt as dirty as his socks had the day before. That Simms had given him trouble two days in a row.

When they reached the corner of Penn and 28th Street, he and Joseph sauntered into Klavon's drugstore and soda fountain and took seats at the dark green marble counter.

"What'll you have, boys? A cherry phosphate? How about a Monongahela River float?" Mr. Klavon wiped his hands on a clean white apron that covered most of him.

"Ice cream cones," Mike said.

The man nodded. "The usual, huh? Having a special today, two scoops for a nickel. How's that sound?" He winked. Mr. Klavon always made deals with them.

"Sounds great," Mike said. The first really good thing that had happened all day. "Strawberry and chocolate for me."

"Same here," Joseph said with a grin. "Except I'd like chocolate first, then strawberry."

"Complicated orders, but I think I can manage." Mr. Klavon turned to the ice cream cooler and reached for a scoop.

Mike and Joseph began to spin on their metal

stools, the tops shaped like giant Coca-Cola bottle caps. They spun slowly at first, then faster and faster. "Three, four, five," Mike counted aloud.

The trick was to see how many times you could spin before Mr. Klavon brought the ice cream cones or you got too dizzy, whichever came first. You had to be careful, though. If you got going too fast, the seat would fly off the base and you could go crashing into the hard marble counter. It had happened once, to Tony.

Joseph counted twelve spins, but Mike topped him at fourteen as Mr. Klavon handed two cones over the counter.

"Hope you're not too spun around to enjoy your ice cream, boys," the shop owner said. "I sell the best ice cream in town. Be a terrible waste if you were to upset your stomachs."

The room still whirled in Mike's eyes, but not so much that he couldn't reach out for his cone and take that first sweet, cold lick of chocolate. Out the window he could see a blur as a pack of younger kids hurried past, arguing among themselves. It reminded him of school. He'd heard *Rat Boy* at least a hundred times today from Simms and his rotten friends.

"It *is* the best ice cream," Mike agreed, taking another quick lick. In spite of everything, he was lucky, he realized. Not only did he have the money to buy such a treat, but Klavon's was only a block from his house, so it was easy to come here. Simms lived somewhere at the other end of the Strip, past St. Patrick's School, and he'd never showed up for a cone, not once. Besides, from the look of him, he didn't have a spare penny for lemon drops, let alone a nickel. *Well, good.*

As if he'd read Mike's mind, Mr. Klavon asked, "Have a nice day in school, boys? Get all your arithmetic problems right?"

"Mostly," Mike replied.

"I did," Joseph said at the same time.

As Mike slurped through the chocolate and into the strawberry, he wished long division were the worst of his problems. But as sweet as the ice cream tasted on his tongue, he still couldn't forget the taunts and whispers that had shadowed him around school all day. *For most kids school means reading, writing and arithmetic,* he thought, *but for me, it's been reading, writing and Rat Boy.*

A slam of the door brought Mike out of his worries. When he turned, he saw Grandpap crossing the scrubbed marble floor toward them. "How you doing Michael? Joseph? Your ice cream cold enough for you?"

Mike grinned. Another good day, if Grandpap could joke around.

Without waiting for an answer, the old man tapped his fingers on the counter.

Mr. Klavon leaned across on his elbows. "What'll it be, Mr. Costa? Milk shake this time? Bet you didn't know it, boys, but this guy used to be famous around here for how fast he could slug down a chocolate malt."

"No malts today, thanks," Grandpap said. He set a

tall green bottle on the counter. "Just fill this up with soda water, if you will, please."

"Stomach bothering you again?" Mr. Klavon asked, all the teasing gone from his voice now.

Mike sat up a little straighter. He knew Grandpap got confused sometimes, but this was the first he'd heard about stomach troubles.

"Just fill her up and I'll be back for one of your malts tomorrow. See if I'm not." Grandpap knocked three times on the counter.

Mr. Klavon turned and held the bottle under the soda spigot until it was full. Then he popped in a cork and passed the bottle back to Grandpap. "Take care, now. Hope you're feeling better soon."

Grandpap took the bottle and reached into his pocket with his other hand, fumbling around. Then he set the bottle down and searched both pockets, his face growing redder and redder as he kept coming up empty.

"Don't worry, Mr. Costa. I'll put it on your tab," Mr. Klavon said. "No point getting agitated. You just go home and tend that stomach of yours." The man hurried out from behind the counter and gave Grandpap his bottle, then helped him to the door.

Mike spun his stool and watched. Best he could tell, Mr. Klavon was pointing the way home, as if Grandpap might get lost. He hoped Joseph didn't notice that. As he turned back to the counter, Mike realized that Grandpap's good day wasn't so good after all.

He probably should have climbed down off his stool and walked the old man home, but that would have meant leaving without finishing his ice cream, or taking a chance of dropping it on the sidewalk if Grandpap got difficult.

Besides, maybe by the time the old man got home, he would have forgotten all about his empty pockets. Holding on to that hope, Mike relaxed and crunched his way through the cone, licking up the sweet strawberry ice cream before it could melt. Maybe tomorrow he'd have Mr. Klavon put the chocolate on the bottom so he could save the best for last.

6

Fish Don't Argue Back

A few minutes later Mike said goodbye to Joseph and walked the single block to number 2905. He shoved open the front door of his house, but before he'd taken three steps, he wished he were still spinning on his bottle cap stool at Klavon's. Grandpap stood in the front room, shouting and waving his arms.

"It's gone, I tell you. Gone. That Tony's taken off with it again."

Mike stepped into the doorway of the front room as if drawn by a magnet. He stopped there and watched, barely able to move.

Grandpap flung a pale green cushion from an

overstuffed chair onto the floor. He moved to the couch and tore off all the back cushions, and the seat cushions as well. Then he turned and dumped the books, even the Bible, from the shelf in the corner. They landed with a hard thump that vibrated through the floor all the way to the soles of Mike's feet.

Mom bustled down the stairs and hurried past Mike. "Now, Grandpap," she began.

"Don't *Now Grandpap* me," the old man said. "That Tony's up to his old tricks. Where is he? Where is he?" His voice rose and filled the room.

"Please, Grandpap," Mom said, taking hold of his left arm. "Just calm down and tell me what's wrong."

Grandpap yanked his arm away. "It's that Tony. He stole my money again. But I'll find it." With that he turned, shoved past Mike and stamped into the hall, heading for the stairs.

Mom followed. She tugged on Mike's arm as the old man mounted the steps. He wasn't very steady on his feet as he climbed, but he made plenty of noise, stamping and muttering all the way up.

Mike obeyed the unspoken command in his mother's firm grip. The two of them would have to stop Grandpap before he got worse.

In the upper hall, Mike caught up to his grand-father and put a hand on his shoulder. "Hi, Grandpap. I'm home from school and I got an A on my spelling test. Want to see?"

"Later. Later." Like a stubborn old bull, Grandpap

lowered his head and charged down the hallway to the room at the end.

The hall was too narrow for Mike or his mother to shove past Grandpap, so all they could do was follow. At the last room Grandpap flung open the door and bellowed out, "Where is it? What have you done with my cash box, you lousy sneak?" He strode into the room.

Once through the doorway, Mike hurried to the side of the bed where his uncle Tony was just sitting up, rubbing his eyes and staring at the old man. "Pop?" Tony mumbled, still partly asleep.

"You get out of bed and find my cash box," Grandpap ordered. "Or else."

"I don't have your cash box, Pop," Tony replied. "We use a cash register now, remember? It stays at the store. Vincent keeps the key, right on his watch chain, remember?"

"None of your lies, Anthony Costa. You think you're so smart, think again. You can't fool me. No, sir, I've been around and I know what's what."

"Go on, Kathleen," Tony said to Mom. "Mike and I will take care of this; you go back downstairs."

With a sigh, Mom turned and left the room, and as she did, Tony climbed out of bed, wearing just his underwear. He flung back the bedcovers and showed them to Grandpap. "Look here, Pop. I got no cash box in the bed, no pockets in my undershirt to hide your money in, no nothing. Vincent's in charge of the money these days. Your oldest son, Vincent."

Tony's voice was firm but to Mike it sounded soft underneath, the way a person would talk to a little kid or a pup. It seemed to get through, because Grandpap stopped arguing and gripped the bottom rail of Tony's bed with both hands. "Vincent? Vincent has the money? Are you sure? Is he old enough to manage our money?"

"Vincent's thirty-three years old, Pop," Tony said. "He's very dependable." Tony's shoulders slumped, as if he were just coming off a long night of lifting crates, as if he hadn't just had eight hours of sleep.

Grandpap turned to Mike with a puzzled frown on his face. "You're not Vincent, then? You're . . ."

"I'm Mike, Grandpap. I'm Mike and I'm twelve. Vincent's my pop. Like Tony says, he's taking good care of your money."

Grandpap heaved a big sigh and shook his head as if trying to clear away the fog that had drifted into his mind. "Sometimes . . . sometimes . . . ," he said.

"It's okay, Grandpap, let's go downstairs and I can show you my spelling paper. Got a hundred percent to-day. Come on." Mike took the old man's arm. He could remember a time when Grandpap had seemed strong and tough, but now his arm felt thin, like bones and skin with no muscles at all. Carefully, Mike steered him back into the hall.

Without warning Grandpap stopped, pulled away from Mike and gripped his stomach with both hands. "My belly's on fire, get out of my way, kid," he shouted, then hurried into the bathroom and slammed the door behind him.

Mike's own stomach felt like it had been pinched from the inside, and all that sweet ice cream sat as heavy as rocks.

Tony stepped closer to Mike and punched him on the shoulder. "Hey, don't take it personal. It's not you he's mad at, it's me."

"I guess," Mike said. "He didn't even know who I was."

"Right, so he isn't mad at you, he's mad at the world."

"But it's my fault. I could have stopped him." Mike explained about Grandpap's visit to Klavon's. "I should have walked him home. I bet I could have calmed him down."

Tony shrugged. "Maybe and maybe not. Seems like the money set him off again. It's happening more and more these days, and often it's money that starts it."

"How come?" Mike asked. "I know times are hard, but we aren't broke, are we?" He sighed. He hadn't planned to ask such a question and probably wouldn't have had the nerve if he'd been talking to Mom or Pop. But Tony was younger and seemed like less of a grown person. So it was easier to ask him.

"Long story. Come on, I'll tell you." Tony steered Mike into his room.

Mike shoved a pile of clothes off an armchair and sat down.

"Times are hard," Tony explained, pacing back and forth between the window and his bed. "But no, we're not broke, not yet anyway. We've got the old man to thank for that. Back in twenty-nine when the crash came the banks started to fold. You remember that?"

Mike nodded. Either he remembered or he remembered hearing about it. You couldn't be alive in 1933 and not know about the crash.

Tony gathered up some clothes and began to get dressed. "My father, your grandpap, he never believed in banks. Kept all his money hidden in little stashes—here around the house, next door with Frank, at the store. So we didn't lose any money in the crash. Sure, business is slow and we're not making a lot, but we've got a cushion."

"If Grandpap knows that, how come he says you've taken his cash box?"

"Well, we did. Sort of. All of us did it, including him," Tony continued, buttoning his shirt. "When a few months had passed and it looked like tough times were here to stay, Pop decided that having all that money here and there might not be safe. Hungry people might turn to thieving. So he dug out all his stashes and split the loot into three piles. One he's got hidden under the floorboards of your parents' room. Another's in the same spot at Frank and Marie's house, and the third he stuck under the bottom shelf of the macaroni wall in the store. That way if a thief comes, or a fire, it won't wipe us out."

"Wow!" Mike said. "How come I didn't know this before?"

"You were just a kid. But you're old enough now. You're part of the business."

Tony was right. Mike *did* work for the family; he took care of the thieving rats. He smiled. "And we're not broke, that's good to know."

"Don't get me wrong, Mike," Tony said slowly. "I won't lie to you, we've had some bad spells during the last four years. Times we had to dip into that cash. We may have to do it again. If we're lucky, the cash will last until these hard times are over. If we're not, maybe I'll have to take another job or something. It probably won't come to that, but who knows?" He shrugged.

Mike thought it over. He didn't like the idea that their luck might not hold. But it was more than luck, he realized, it was brains. Grandpap had been smart back then, really smart, which made it even harder when his mind got all twisted up now. "Are you sure that's the money he was talking about today? I know he said 'cash box,' but he'd also been looking for change to pay Mr. Klavon."

"I don't know for sure," Tony said. "Could be that any mention of money makes him confused. Shoot, a few minutes ago I'd have sworn he was yelling at his brother Tony, not me, and *that* Tony's been dead for fifteen years." He sighed and his shoulders slumped. "I just wish he knew who I was. . . ."

"He knows," Mike began, "deep down—"

"Look, Mike," Tony interrupted, "these days, I'm not sure your grandpap even has a deep-down place left."

"Sometimes he does," Mike said loudly, as if saying so would make it true. Sure, his grandfather made him mad sometimes, but he hated it when people said mean things. "Today's just a bad day."

Before Tony could disagree, the bathroom door opened and Grandpap stormed out. "You men there, what are you doing? Get your clothes on and go about your business. I don't pay my employees to stand around shooting the breeze." He swiped a hand across his mouth.

"But Pop—" Tony began.

"No arguments. I'm tired of all the back talk, so just shut up, both of you. I'm getting my fishing pole and catching some catfish. The fish, they don't argue back." He paused and glared at Mike. "And when I come home, you men had better be back to work. Understand?"

He turned and stamped down the stairs, still muttering.

The only words Mike could make out were *lazy* and *sneaks*. And the rocks in his stomach grew bigger and bigger.

7

Empty Traps and Dead Rats

Early the next morning Mike checked the cellar of the warehouse. Again he found empty traps in all four corners. Strange. One of the traps near the loading dock was full, though, and he dumped it into his pail. Unless he found a couple more dead rats, there'd be no ice cream, only a sack of penny candy. What a dirty deal.

When he reached the other side of the dock, his stomach turned and thoughts of ice cream melted away. The head of a small gray mouse lay wedged under the snapping bar of the big rattrap, but the body had been flung off to the side by the force of the spring. It wasn't the first time Mike had seen such a thing, but he sure didn't like it. He picked up the trap, nudging the small gray body with his shoe until he could dump it into the pail.

After finding that, he nearly called it quits for the day, but there were still two traps under the stairs to check. If either of them was full, by tomorrow the whole cellar would stink. Taking a deep breath, he stepped toward the back wall. A quick glance showed that those traps too stood empty. When he bent to look more closely, he noticed that both traps had been sprung and the bait was gone.

"Darn it," Mike muttered. Every now and then they got a smart rat in the cellar, one who could spring the traps and steal the bait without getting caught. Mike wasn't about to let that continue.

He called out in a loud voice, "So, we've got a sneak thief, have we? We'll see about that." Still talking to himself, he tossed the two sprung traps into his pail so he could rebait them.

The memory of that headless mouse made him decide to dump the carcasses before replacing the hunks of cheese rind. He slid open the door to the outside and was about to step onto the loading dock when he noticed that his father and three uncles were huddling together, deep in conversation. Uncle Frank was talking, and Pop had a serious look on his face.

Clutching his pail, Mike stepped out quietly and listened.

"I didn't want to bring it up last night in front of the old man," Uncle Frank said. "He'll just stew about it and get confused. And your Kathleen has enough to do, keeping an eye on him all day long, without him getting more agitated."

"Are you sure Sal's really shutting down?" Tony asked. He caught sight of Mike and shot him a quick wink but didn't give him away to the others.

Uncle Frank nodded, a grim scowl on his face. "Sal told me himself. He can't make a go of it, can't keep up with the rent. So he's closing down his store, selling off his goods and just giving up. He's going to go live with his wife's family."

Mike's heart thumped loudly as his uncle's words began to fit together. *No!* Another small grocery store was closing. One less customer for Costa Brothers. Five or six of their customers had gone bust during the past year and it had Pop plenty worried. Mike had seen him sitting at the kitchen table late at night writing numbers in his account books and then shaking his head and frowning. So in spite of what Tony had told him about hidden money . . .

"Hey, look on the bright side, the folks in Bloomfield still gotta eat. Maybe our orders will go up at the other two markets." That was Roberto, always trying to find the good side.

Uncle Frank shook his head. "Yeah, and maybe Mr. Franklin Delano Roosevelt's gonna come out to Pittsburgh and put a hundred-dollar bill in every man's pocket too. Wise up, Roberto, we're in the middle of a depression. Times are bad and getting worse."

As he heard the words, Mike couldn't help seeing

the thin gray faces of the men who huddled in Father Cox's churchyard waiting for a handout of soup. That couldn't happen to their family, could it? His grip on the handle of the pail tightened.

"I could look for a daytime job," Tony offered. "I'm young, I'm plenty strong. Might bring in some extra cash . . ."

"Now, boys," Pop began, "Franco's right, times are hard. But I think we've hit bottom already. I think our new president is going to get the country working again. We just need to give him time. Meanwhile, we'll tighten our belts a little."

"But, Vince, we're already running as tight as we can," Uncle Frank said. "We gotta pay our suppliers, pay gas on the truck . . ."

Darn it anyway, Mike thought. This might turn into one of those times they'd have to dip into that hidden cash. And every time they did that, there'd be less left for the time after.

Pop clapped an arm around Uncle Frank. "Hey, we're rich compared to most guys. We eat three squares a day. We own our houses and our store, so no landlord's going to toss us on the street. So what if we cut down on the meat at lunch? Hey, macaroni's cheap. We got a warehouse full of food and a cellar full of coal; we won't starve and we won't freeze."

With that, the uncles went back to their unloading and Mike slipped inside. As he knelt to rebait the four traps, he didn't even bother chopping off the tail of the one rat he'd caught; he just dumped it and the mouse into the quicklime pit. Maybe it was a good thing he hadn't caught a lot today. He didn't want Pop to have to take out a cent of that saved-up money. If the business was in trouble, he'd have to find another way to earn money for ice cream, or else go without.

As Mike headed up Penn Avenue toward school, he tried to imagine what it might feel like to hold a hundred-dollar bill in his hand. He wondered how many ice cream cones and milk shakes a guy could buy with so much money. He wanted to believe Pop, believe that the new president would make things better. And he wanted it to happen fast, before any more grocery stores stopped buying from Costa Brothers.

Joseph was waiting for him at the corner of 19th Street, poking at something in the gutter with a slat from an orange crate. "You catch any of these today?" Joseph asked. He nudged at the gutter again and Mike saw a dead rat. "Here's one you missed."

At Joseph's prodding, the rat's body rolled over and Mike could see its belly, bloated and swollen. He looked away. "I didn't catch much," he said carefully. He didn't want to spill the beans about the family business. "Just one rat and a puny little mouse. The trap was so strong it chopped the mouse's head clean off."

"Nasty," Joseph replied, but he was grinning. "Should have saved that for old Simms."

"Should have. But I'll tell you what else," Mike said. "We've got a sneak thief in the cellar. A tricky old rat sprang two traps and stole the bait. I'm gonna catch that fella, just you wait. . . ."

As they neared 17th Street and Father Cox's church, Mike forced himself to look at the glassy eyes of dead fish, arranged in rows on ice in the windows of the fish market on the opposite side of the street. The last thing he needed was to see those hobos and be reminded of how bad things were getting in the country.

"Hey, look at this. Another dead rat." Joseph stopped and squatted, peering at a shadowy form that lay alongside a brick building. "Maybe you aren't catching a lot 'cause the rats are dying on their own. That plus your thief stealing your bait could really cut into your profits."

"Yeah, maybe." Mike bent to take a closer look, then stepped back. The rat gave off a heavy, rotten smell, like it had been dead awhile.

Mike shook his head. Tramps and hobos on one side of the street, dead rats on the other. No matter where he looked, he saw something ugly. Maybe Uncle Frank was right after all; things were bad and getting worse.

8

The Fight

The boys hurried along the sidewalks, covering the remaining three blocks nearly at a run. A good thing too, because the warning bell rang as they pushed open the front door.

Racing stiff-legged so they wouldn't get caught running in the halls, Mike led the way upstairs. The second bell sounded as he slid into his seat and he breathed heavily. Not late, but almost. What he saw next, though, made him stop breathing entirely for a moment.

Somebody had stuck a hand-drawn picture of a rat on the top of his desk. The rat was long and black, with pointy teeth that showed in a mean snarl. And the thick curling tail reminded Mike of a black snake. Underneath, someone had scrawled "Costa Brothers' Sausages, Made with the Finest Ingredients."

Mike wadded up the paper, then spun around. He could see an ugly grin on the face of Andy Simms. "You just wait, Simms, you just wait," he muttered, curling the fingers of his right hand into a fist. Lunch recess couldn't come soon enough.

Mike only gave half his attention to the rows of long division, earning himself a C-minus when they traded their papers and checked answers. He didn't do much better on the grammar exercises. As the morning wore on, his temper simmered, building to a fury by noontime.

"You take it back!" Mike shouted when he finally ran from the classroom and cornered Andy Simms at the far wall of the playground.

"I won't," Simms replied, "because it's true. The Costa brothers grind up dead rats and add them to their sausages. Then they put in all those hot I-talian spices so nobody knows."

"That's a dirty lie!" Mike yelled. He had to shut Simms' mouth. Pop's business was already in trouble with the times so bad. If Simms repeated his stories, nobody would buy from Mike's family and they'd all go broke.

Out of the corner of his eye, he could see Joseph approaching. Then three of Simms' friends stepped up with scowls on their ugly mugs.

"Prove it, Rat Boy," Simms said as his pals stationed themselves on either side of him with their backs to the rough brick wall.

"You bet," Mike said.

The fury that had been simmering inside all morning exploded. He hauled back and swung, planting a good solid smack right on Simms' nose. It felt great, so he slugged him again, on the cheek.

Simms let fly with both fists, hammering away at Mike's face and ears.

Mike gave it back, swing for swing, blow for blow. He could feel his muscles sing as he fought. Andy's pounding didn't seem to hurt or even slow him down; instead it just made Mike aim better and hit harder. After a while he was hitting any face that got close enough. *Slam! That one's for Pop. Slam! That's for Tony.*

Dust rose on the playground and he tasted blood in his mouth, but he didn't let that stop him. Then strong arms were pulling him, yanking him away from Simms. The next thing he knew, he and several others were lined up along a wall in Sister Mary Theodore's office. And the principal was carrying her famous wooden ruler, which had set fire to the backsides of hundreds of guys, Mike included. They were in for it now.

Mike sniffed and wiped blood from the corner of his mouth. From the lineup, he saw that he and Joseph had taken on Simms and three grubby pals, outnumbered four to two. And they'd held their own, from the looks of the other boys' faces. Simms' left eye was swelling up; Mike rubbed his right knuckles against the side of his shirt, polishing them.

He didn't dare look too proud, though, for Sister Mary Ted was pacing up and down along the row, smacking that ruler against her palm and glaring at each dirty face. "I suppose you ruffians have some sort of explanation for this," she began. "It had better be good." She stopped right in front of Simms, who pointed at Mike.

"He started it, Sister. I was just minding my own business on the playground and he came over and pounded me."

Sister Mary Ted cocked her head to one side and frowned, glancing up and down the row of boys. She settled on Simms' shifty-eyed friends. "And you three, what's your excuse?"

"We saw Costa go after Andy Simms. We were just helping out."

So that's how it's going to be, Mike thought. *I'm going to get all the blame unless I tell about the rat picture. But if I do, more people will hear what Simms is saying about Costa Brothers, and that stinks. Guess I'll take my knocks and get it over with, but no squealing. No matter what Sister does, we still beat them in the fight.*

When Sister stopped in front of him, he could feel a coldness, like the coldness of the ice he'd seen in the fish market that morning, shoot out at him from her pale green eyes. Darn, why couldn't Sisters wear ordinary clothes and have hair? They wouldn't look so spooky then.

"Well, Michael Costa?"

"No, Sister, no reason. Just a fight."

Joseph shrugged, but at least he had the sense to say, "Sorry, Sister. Won't happen again."

"See that it doesn't." She paced in front of them twice more and Mike was imagining how many whacks they'd each get when she stopped again right in front of him.

"I had thought to give you each ten stripes," she said, as if reading his mind. "But that hasn't worked in the past. Instead, you will all spend the afternoon here in my office, doing your schoolwork in absolute quiet."

A couple of guys groaned, but Sister silenced them with one of her sharp, frowning glares. Sister was famous for those. Mike figured that was why the school had picked her as principal—that and the ruler.

"As I said," she continued, her voice as sharp as the glare had been, "you will work in absolute silence. Then, when classes are dismissed for the day, you'll help Mr. Murray clean the entire building, including the washrooms."

Oh, great, Mike thought. But he kept it to himself.

Sister tapped a pencil on a stack of papers on her desk. "I'm sending a note to each of your families, explaining why you'll be arriving home late today. I assume they will show you exactly how disappointed they are by your behavior. And on Saturday, each of you will have plenty to say at confession."

Six heads wobbled briefly, Mike's included, as he

wondered who'd get the note. If there was anything fair in this world, Grandpap would be the one and he'd forget all about it. But the way things were going, Mom would get it and she'd take up where Sister Mary Ted had left off. He'd be lucky if he got anything except bread and water to eat, and it would probably take at least a week for him to be able to sit down once Mom finished with him.

From one until three Mike slogged through his history and geography books and wrote out definitions for twenty-five new vocabulary words in silence. Even Simms and his friends weren't dumb enough to disobey Sister Mary Ted's orders.

From three until six he pushed a broom and a mop, and his rotten luck held. Mr. Murray had them draw lots to see who would clean what, and Mike got last pick, so he had to clean up first grade and the younger boys' washroom. And those little stinkers missed the toilets more than they hit them, so he had to mop that floor twice.

But as he mopped, Mike told himself over and over again, *we won. It was a fair fight, and we were outnumbered, but the good guys won.* Best of all, the whole school had watched him pound on Andy Simms. What was a little mopping, compared to that?

9

You've Got to Be Tough

When Mike reached home that evening it was already dusky outside. He wanted nothing more than a chance to soak away his sore, achy places in a hot bathtub and to try to clean up the muck he knew covered his face. But Mom was waiting for him in the parlor.

"Well, young man," she said as he walked through the front door. "You've shamed the entire family. What's the meaning of this?"

"I . . . I got in a fight, that's all. Wasn't my fault. Darn that Andy Simms anyway; he started it."

"I've heard that line before. He couldn't have started anything if you'd walked away, mister. What happened?"

"What happened?" Grandpap echoed, stepping carefully into the parlor. "Looks like somebody popped you one right in the nose. Break any bones?"

"I don't think so, Grandpap."

Grandpap stepped closer and studied Mike's face. "Did you give him back what for? You're not going to let some bully pick on you, are you?"

"No, sir. I socked him. Gave him a shiner too."

"Good for you, Michael."

"Grandpap!" Mom scolded. "Giving somebody a shiner is not a good thing. Now what happened?"

Mike didn't want to get into all the details, the name-calling and the rat picture, not with Mom. "They were saying things about our sausage. . . ."

"You got into a fight about sausage? That's the most ridiculous thing I ever—"

"Now slow down, Kathleen," Grandpap said. "You women don't understand such things."

"I'll tell you what I understand," Mom said, her voice low and tight. She tugged on the shoulder of Mike's shirt and he noticed a good-sized rip. "I'm the one who has to patch this shirt and wash out the bloodstains. And it was a new shirt too. You're not get-ting another just because you tore this one." She let out a big breath and stomped off toward the kitchen.

"Thanks, Grandpap," Mike said. "I'm glad you took my side."

"Women just don't understand," the old man re-peated. "A man's got to be tough. I remember a time I got into quite a scuffle myself. Couldn't have been much older than you are either. Me and my brother Tony paired up against three Valencia boys, all bigger than we were. How many did you fight?"

"There were four of them against just Joseph and me and we plastered them."

"Good job. Want to put some beefsteak on that nose of yours?"

"Nah," Mike said. He pointed toward the kitchen. "Beefsteak costs too much and I don't want to ask Mom. She'll just holler again."

"Yep. She will. My ma lit into Tony and me after we whupped those Valencia boys. Five of them, maybe six; all I remember was having sore knuckles from the punches I threw." Grandpap raised his fists and punched the air, grinning. Then his hands went to his belly and he turned.

"What is it, Grandpap? What's wrong?"

"Bathroom. Hurry."

Mike half-shoved him up the stairs and into the bathroom. He reached to lift up the toilet lid, but not in time. Grandpap leaned over the bathtub and heaved. Mike's stomach twisted and he looked away, but he could feel Grandpap's arm trembling, so he held on. A sour smell filled the room. Three more times Grandpap emptied his belly; then he swayed from side to side.

Mike helped him toward the toilet. "Come on, sit down here, on the seat. I'll get Mom."

"No. Don't tell on me. She'll just fret." Sharp fingers gripped Mike's arm. "A man's got to be tough."

"But Grandpap . . ."

"Let me just sit here. This will pass, if I sit quiet. Usually does."

"What do you mean 'usually'?" Mike asked. "Do you get sick like this a lot?"

"Sick, what do you mean sick?" Grandpap's head snapped up and he was scowling. "I've never been sick a day in my life and don't you forget it."

"But Grandpap . . ."

"Listen to your elders, son. I'm going to go down and tune in to some boxing on the radio before supper." He stood and made his way out the door and down the hallway toward the stairs.

Mike hurried to the window and threw it open, welcoming the cold fresh air. After sucking in several deep, sweet breaths, he switched on the lightbulb over the sink, trying to decide whether to tell Mom about Grandpap or just clean up the mess himself.

The old man was right; Mom would fuss, he thought. And she was mad at Mike already, so maybe he'd just clean it up and see what happened next. He reached for a pail and turned on the spigot to fill it. Then he looked into the bathtub.

Holding his breath, Mike looked closer. He could swear he was seeing more than vomit. Unless he was mistaken, and please, yes, he'd love to be mistaken about this. But no, his eyes weren't deceiving him. Dark red stains streaked the white tub.

Grandpap was vomiting blood.

10

Bananas

Mike figured the supper table was the worst place to bring up Grandpap's sickness. He decided to wait till afterward, when he could talk to just Mom and Pop without spoiling anybody's appetite. As it turned out, Mom spoiled his by bringing up the fight again.

"Our Michael got into another brawl at school today," she announced as they passed around a platter of spaghetti and meatballs.

"I kinda wondered about that," Tony said, winking at Mike. "Looks like you took one on the nose, kid. Is it busted?"

"I can breathe okay," Mike said. He helped himself

to a plateful of spaghetti, then spooned some onto Grandpap's plate. "Doesn't hurt too bad."

"Was it a fair fight? Did you win or lose?" Pop asked.

"Vincent, what sort of questions are those?" Mom demanded. "This boy needs a talking-to."

"I *was* talking to him, Kathleen." Pop turned to Mike. "Well, did the kid deserve it? Did you win or lose?"

Mom made a *tsk*ing sound, but none of the men around the table seemed to pay attention, so Mike figured he'd better answer Pop.

"He deserved it, and we came out even," Mike explained. "Everybody looked about as banged up as me when it was over."

"How many everybodies you talking about?" Pop asked.

"Two of us, four of them." Mike tried hard not to make it sound like bragging so Mom wouldn't start in again.

"Sounds like a victory to me," Tony said. "Good job, kid. I suppose the Sisters raised a fuss. They always caught me after a good one."

"Yep. We all had to stay after and clean the school. Even the washrooms." Mike wrinkled his sore nose, remembering the smell.

"Well, then." Pop nodded and broke off a hunk of bread. "I'd say you paid for your mischief. Next time don't let them gang up on you."

"Next time!" Mom's words slammed across the table, and Mike was relieved. It seemed like she was madder at Pop and Tony than at him. "There'd better not be a next time!"

"Now, Kathleen, boys will get into scrapes now and then. The important thing is coming out on top."

"Don't you tell me what boys will or won't do." Mom stood and stormed off to the stove, carrying the empty spaghetti platter.

Tony winked at Mike and spoke softly. "I'd say you got your temper honestly, Mike. Fire from your mother's redheaded Irish side, and thunder from us."

"You got a kid picking on you, you let him have it, hear? He gives you five punches, give him ten," Pop whispered behind Mom's back. "But next time, don't get into a fight on school time. And stop by the warehouse to clean up before you come home. That way your mother won't scold."

"I just wish I had a couple of brothers," Mike grumbled. "Then they'd get some of the scolding and I wouldn't get stuck with it all. How about it, Pop? No sisters, but a couple of little brothers would be great."

"Michael, Michael," Pop began, shaking his head.

BAM!!!

Whatever Pop was going to say got drowned out by a huge boom that rattled the kitchen windows and thrummed in Mike's chest. Mom spun around. Pop, Tony, Grandpap and Mike all jumped up from the table.

"What was that?" Mike shouted.

"An explosion," Pop said. "Sounded like it came from the street."

Tony was already grabbing his jacket from the hook by the back door; Mike followed right on his heels. Pop and Grandpap tugged on their coats, and Mom did too.

As they spilled outside, Aunt Marie, Uncle Frank and Roberto rushed out from the house next door. People were already hurrying up Penn Avenue and the Costa family joined the crowd. As he ran, Mike caught an odd scent in the air. A burning smell, but sweet too. Almost like bananas. The minute he smelled it, a murmur rose from the crowd. "Bananas? Bananas?"

As if people were being pulled by their noses, they all turned down 28th Street toward Smallman, where the banana warehouse stood. Sure enough, the closer Mike got to the corner of 22nd and Smallman, the stronger the smell was.

When he reached the block of the warehouse, Mike noticed that most of the buildings now had jagged holes where glass windows were supposed to be.

"Tony, Roberto, go check our building," Pop ordered. "See if the front window is busted."

Mike was tempted to tag along, but he wanted to see what had happened. Around him the crowd grew thick and some men began shoving people back, away from the banana warehouse. "Watch out, now, watch out for fire. Stand back, don't get too close."

By the glow of the streetlights, Mike could see smoke rising into the sky. Bananas, ripe ones and green ones, lay everywhere, some smashed, some still in neat bunches.

As his eyes grew used to the smoke, he noticed St. Stanislaus, the church across the street from the warehouse. Its windows had all blown out and the two gold domes on the roof were blackened and tipped to one side. The rest of the roof looked like it was covered in mashed bananas. *Man, what a boom!*

Mike shoved between the men and women who crowded the sidewalk and wriggled his way through until he could see the section of the warehouse that the smoke was coming from. When he got as close as he could, the thick smoke stung his throat. He found Joseph squirming to the front for a good look too.

"Come on, let's try around back," Joseph said. "We might see more."

Mike nodded and tried not to cough, but as they turned, sirens blared through the night air and the fire trucks arrived. Firemen set up their hoses, and soon pumpers were spraying the warehouse with high arching streams of water. When the smoke cleared, Mike could see a huge hole along one side of the building.

"Look at that. Something blew out the whole brick wall!" He turned to Joseph.

"I never knew bananas were so tough," Joseph said, picking up an undamaged green one. "What do you think caused it?"

"I don't know, dynamite maybe. Is your father on duty tonight?"

"Pop threw on his uniform soon as we heard the

boom," Joseph said. "The minute he knows something, I'll tell you."

As the firemen finished hosing down the building and began to look inside, Mike could hear some people around them talking. "Wonder if one of those dirty bums over by the church had something to do with it?" a woman said.

"It's all over now, folks, time to go home. We gotta clean up this mess." Cops herded the crowd away from the corner and back toward Penn Avenue. As people were leaving, firemen turned their hoses on the street.

Mike jumped back so his shoes wouldn't get drenched, and he caught sight of Joseph's pop helping to move the crowd. "Watch your step, now, these bananas can be slippery. Time to go home, everybody. Time to go home."

"We better scram so the firemen can clean the streets," Joseph said. "See you tomorrow."

"Yeah, tomorrow." Mike turned and headed back toward Penn Avenue and Costa Brothers.

By the next day the cops might know more about who had blown up the bananas, and even if they didn't, he and Joseph could snoop out the truth. Who could say, they might even find an exploded tarantula from one of those banana crates.

When Mike reached Penn Avenue he found his uncles Tony and Roberto hammering wide boards over what had been the front window of the warehouse. "Need any help?"

"Nah, we're nearly done," Roberto said. "I don't

want to be the one to tell Franco about it, though. This is going to cost a pretty penny to fix. A penny we don't have."

"Lucky thing Vince sent us over right away, though," Tony added. "Could have been worse. Look– across the street."

Mike turned and stared at Slawski's Fruit Market, directly across Penn Avenue from Costa Brothers. A bunch of men–they looked like hobos–were helping themselves to crates full of apples and oranges.

"Bad enough we've got to buy a new window," Roberto said as he hammered a nail with two hard whacks. "At least we didn't lose any of our goods. Franco would really pop his cork if that ever happened to us."

"He sure would," Mike said. But deep down, he wondered about those hobos. Was it possible some of them had set off the explosion just to steal some ba- nanas? Could a person get that hungry?

When Mike reached home, Pop was sitting on the front steps waiting, so Mike sat down next to him. "I heard somebody say the hobos might have blown up the bananas. What do you think, Pop?"

"I think that's a lousy thing to say." Pop looked Mike right in the eye. "Sure, some of those fellas might get into mischief once in a while, like anybody, but mostly they're just ordinary men. Broke, hungry and down on their luck, but not criminals. I don't want you repeating such cheap talk."

"I won't," Mike agreed. He hadn't much liked the

sound of it himself, even though the hobos did give him the willies sometimes.

"While we're on the subject, there's something else I don't want to hear again. You've got to stop asking for brothers. You're breaking your mother's heart, Michael."

"But, Pop, that's no fair. You got three brothers. Even the business, it's called Costa Brothers. Being the only kid isn't much fun."

"I understand that. Now, here's something you need to understand. I haven't told you this before because you were too young. But now you're old enough, so we've got to talk. Man to man. I'm going to tell you this once and I expect it to stick."

Mike swallowed. He wasn't sure he wanted to hear what Pop was about to say, but he didn't have much choice.

"Your mother and I, we'd like to have more kids too. Boys, girls, some of each. Every couple of years since you were born, your mom's gotten started on a baby. But then something always goes wrong."

"How can that be?" Mike interrupted. "I'm not a little kid, you know. I notice things. Look at Aunt Marie. Women get fat when babies are on the way and I've never seen Mom fat."

Pop shook his head in the saddest way and Mike knew Pop was telling him the truth flat out.

"Babies grow kinda slow, Mike. Your mother always has her troubles early, before she has a chance to grow a big belly, so you wouldn't notice anything. But she gets . . . We both get sad for a while. With you asking all the time, it makes things worse."

Mike sat there feeling like a dummy. He rubbed his arms; somehow the cold air seemed to leak through his coat.

"I'm not telling you this so you can spread it around the neighborhood, now," Pop said. "I'm telling you for two reasons. First, so you'll shut your trap about having brothers—you'll just have to make do with a cousin when Aunt Marie hatches you one. Second, you need to understand that your mother has hard times, sad times. So we've gotta be extra nice to her. You especially. Since you're the only kid she's likely to have, you gotta be a good one."

Mike ducked away from Pop's words. He felt like a crate loaded with watermelons had just landed on his shoulders. "No fair," he said. "That's not how I want it to be."

"I know." Pop put his arm around Mike's shoulder. "Even when you grow up, life's not always fair. You don't always get what you want. Think of those hobos. All they want is a job, a chance to put food on the table—but no dice."

With that, Pop stood and left Mike sitting on the front steps feeling colder than ever. And more alone than ever.

11

Hobos

Joseph arrived a few minutes after nine o'clock on Saturday morning, wearing a grin that told Mike he had news. Now he was sitting in the old brown easy chair, slumped down in the sagging seat.

Joseph was just what Mike needed to blow away the shadows that had haunted his sleep all night. "Tell me! Tell me!" he demanded, plopping onto the narrow bed in his attic room. "Who blew up the bananas?"

"They don't know *who* yet, but they do know *how*."

"Okay, tell me how."

"It's complicated," Joseph began. "You know how the bananas look when they come off the boxcars?"

"Yeah . . ."

"So hard they'd wear out your jaw if you tried to eat one."

Mike nodded. He could remember biting into a banana that was only slightly green. It had left the backs of his teeth feeling fuzzy, like caterpillars. One of those deep green bananas would taste terrible. "What do green bananas have to do with the explosion?"

"My pop and his partner interviewed the guys at the warehouse and they explained it all. One of their jobs is to take those green bananas and turn them into ripe ones real quick."

"How do they do that?"

Joseph laughed. "They lock them up in a room with no windows. Kinda like putting the bananas in jail, you know? And then they gas them, with a special invisible gas . . . ethylene, I think Pop called it."

"For real?"

"Cross my heart," Joseph said, swiping his hand across his chest. "Anyway, remember the part of the warehouse where the wall blew out? That was the ripening room—the part that exploded. The guy told my pop something probably made a spark and that room full of gas just blew sky high. . . ."

"Busting out the wall, breaking windows all over and knocking over the domes at St. Stan's church," Mike finished. "Wow! Any idea what made the spark?"

"That's what they're trying to figure out today. Pop and his partner are going door to door, asking folks if they saw anybody suspicious just before the blast."

Mike frowned. "But the Strip is so crowded, people

are always walking around. How could they find the right person?"

"It's not crowded at suppertime, just at night. All the food trains come in around midnight, so when it gets late, the place is hopping. But by the middle of the afternoon, everybody's in bed, resting up for the next night's work."

Mike felt dumb; he knew all this stuff too. He probably knew it better than Joseph; he just hadn't been thinking straight. "Okay. So they'll go door to door and ask questions. And find the guy who did it. What do you think? A gangster maybe?" Mike grinned. "I know, Pretty Boy Floyd breezed into Pittsburgh and decided to hold up a banana warehouse. He busted in the door and waved his guns around. *This is a stickup. One wrong move and you're banana cream pie!*"

"Right," Joseph said, "and then one brave banana tried to save them all, but Pretty Boy shot him and the whole place blew up."

Mike and Joseph started to laugh and couldn't stop. When Mike could finally catch his breath again, his stomach ached so bad, he might as well have eaten one of those nasty green bananas.

"I don't know," Joseph said at last. "I think Pretty Boy holds up banks, not bananas. He likes cash."

"Okay, all we have to do is figure out who likes bananas."

"That's easy. Monkeys. Apes. Gorillas." Joseph sat forward in his chair and puffed out his chest, scratching at his sides.

"I know," Mike said. "It was gangster gorillas. A whole mob of them. They escaped from the zoo and sneaked down to the Strip to rob the warehouse."

Joseph nodded. "But one of the gorillas was dumb and he was smoking a big old fat cigar, and when he walked in the door, the cigar hit the gas and *boom!*"

More laughter. Just under the laughing, Mike could feel worry nudging at his mind, but he couldn't quite grab hold of it. "It doesn't seem like a person or even a gorilla could have busted into that room and started the explosion—at least not without getting hurt himself. Did your pop or one of the other cops find anybody hurt?"

"Nope. Not yet. Right now they're calling it an accident. But they might change their tune after they go door to door today."

I should tell Joseph's pop about the hobos, about how they were stealing fruit from Slawski's last night. Maybe they blew up the banana warehouse. But maybe they didn't; maybe they just saw a broken window and helped themselves. Old Man Slawski will tell anyway; the cops will believe him more than they'll believe a kid.

Mike shook his head, trying to shove the suspicious thoughts out of his mind. Yes, those jobless men were rough and dirty and wore raggedy clothes, but they were just down on their luck, not bums, not bad guys. Mike swallowed hard and hoped it was true.

Later, after Joseph had gone home, and after Mom had made a nice hot lunch, Mike decided to tell her about Grandpap being sick the night before. In the excitement of the explosion, Grandpap's troubles had just plain jumped out of his mind. Pop's man-to-man talk had shoved them even farther away.

Now that Mike remembered, he needed to tell somebody, to get it off his chest. After what Pop had told him, the thought of talking to Mom about something so serious made him nervous, though. He didn't want to make her sad again; still, he had to tell somebody about Grandpap. He waited until the old man had finished eating and had gone into the parlor to switch on the radio.

"You want some help with the dishes?" Mike began. "I'll dry."

"Sure. Thanks." Mom tilted her head to one side and studied his face. "You have something on your mind, Michael?"

"Yeah. Last night before supper."

"You were telling me about the fight at school." Mom plugged up the sink and turned on the water.

"Yeah, I'm sorry about that, but that's not what I want to talk about. It's Grandpap. After you went off to cook supper last night, he started telling me about when he was a boy and got into fights."

"You men and your fights, sometimes you just wear me out. The way you tell it, a fight is something to brag about. My brothers always acted that way too." Mom's cheeks turned pink and Mike could tell she was getting mad all over again. "Mark my words, Michael Costa. A day will come when you're in a tough spot—a spot so tough you won't know how to get out of it—and fighting won't help. It will only make things worse."

Oh boy, Mom had started in on one of her sermons.

"Please, Mom. I'm not bragging, honest. I'm worried. I need to tell you something. It's important."

"Okay. I'll hear you out." She passed him a rinsed plate.

Mike took it and began to dry. "Like I said, one minute Grandpap was telling me about when he was a boy. The next, he was holding his belly and rushing to the bathroom."

"He has been complaining about stomach pains," Mom said. "But that's the least of his problems these days. I know you worry about him, Mike. We all do. It's hard to see a strong man like Grandpap forget where he is. Some days I think he even forgets *who* he is. That's the saddest of all."

Mutely, Mike nodded. If he tried to say anything he'd probably bust out and cry.

Mom put her arm around Mike's shoulder and gave him a quick, damp squeeze. "I know you and your grandpap have always been close. And I wish you didn't have to see him coming apart at the seams. But there's not much we can do. The fact is, I think the complaining is just part of his other trouble. You know, in his mind . . ."

Mike took a deep breath. "It's more than complaining, Mom. He heaved up his toenails. Got sick three or four times."

"What? Why didn't you come get me?" The plate she was washing slid back down into the soapsuds.

"I wanted to, but he said don't. You'd just fuss. I was going to tell you and Pop last night, but when the bananas exploded, I forgot."

"Of course I'd fuss. Somebody's supposed to fuss if a person gets sick four times. Men!"

"Mom. There's more," Mike said. "When I cleaned it up, well, there was blood. Not just vomit." Mike felt his shoulders slump. It was a relief to tell somebody, to let Mom take over the worries.

"You sure?" Mom gripped the edge of the sink and looked hard at Mike.

"I think so. It was red."

"Could have been ketchup from the meatloaf sandwich he had for lunch yesterday. Not that I'm doubting you. But Grandpap's difficult. He needs a lot of attention. And he doesn't always remember if he has eaten or not. I've caught him in the kitchen, not a half hour after lunch, and he's eating a second meal. Maybe that's what happened yesterday. Maybe he just got too full and had to empty his stomach."

"Maybe. But I don't think so. Something he said made me think he's been sick like that before. Will you talk to Pop about it? Please? Will you take Grandpap to the doctor?"

Mom shook her head. "You know how he is about doctors. I doubt we can get him to go. But I will talk to your father. We'll watch Grandpap more closely."

"Promise?"

"I promise. And I'd like your help, Mike. It wouldn't hurt you to spend more time at home keeping an eye on Grandpap and less time on the street fighting."

Mike frowned, but he didn't argue. Maybe this would be a way to help Mom, to make up for all the times he'd asked for brothers. "Sure, Mom, whatever you say."

12

Costa Brothers

By Monday, when Mike followed Pop and Uncle Frank up Penn Avenue to the warehouse, he was mightily tired of the stench of bananas. The fire companies had done their best, hosing down the buildings and streets with river water, but a sweet, rotting smell still hung like a cloud over the Strip. It would take a good rain to wash away the last of those slimy bananas, Mike figured, and it couldn't happen soon enough for him.

Suspicion clouded the air as well. After two days of questioning, all the cops had been able to find out was that a man had been seen sneaking around the warehouse just a few minutes before the explosion. Some

72

folks claimed it was one of Father Cox's hobos looking for food. Others—the cops included, according to Joseph—said it was just an unknown man.

When he reached the warehouse cellar that Monday morning, Mike found empty traps, several sprung with the bait stolen. That sneaky rat was at it again. "I didn't catch anything," he complained to Pop after resetting the traps. "Seems like most of the rats have disappeared."

"Maybe they have," Pop agreed. "We're so close to the banana warehouse, they're probably filling up on those blown-up bananas. I saw a couple out there yesterday, looking full and happy."

At the thought, the inside of Mike's mouth felt like it was covered with scum. Before this had happened, he'd liked bananas, especially banana splits. But if he never saw or smelled a banana again, it would be just fine.

Hope a big rain comes soon, Mike thought as he stepped out onto Penn Avenue. *Or else nobody will eat the cheese in my traps and I'll be broke, just like the hobos. No, that's not right,* he decided with a shake of his head. The Costa family could never be in that bad shape, not even if Pop's business was in trouble; at least, he hoped not. They still had the hidden cash supply, which had to count for something.

By the time he and Joseph got to school, Mike figured, the stench of bananas should have nearly disappeared. Instead, as they neared the gate to the schoolyard, the smell grew stronger than ever.

"Do you believe that?" Joseph said, peering through the fence. "Somebody's been busy. Look— mush and bananas everywhere."

Mike scowled at the scene in front of him. Rotting bananas and slimy goo covered the ground. Sister Mary Ted and a couple of the teachers were standing in a corner holding their skirts off the ground and poking into a trash can.

Other teachers—including Mike's—worked beside the front door, spreading out newspapers to make a path from the sidewalk. Behind Mike, more and more kids were arriving and peering through the fence. Finally Sister Mary John brushed off her hands. "All right, boys and girls. Walk carefully, now. Stay on the newspapers so you don't track up the school."

"Yes, Sister. We will, Sister," the kids milling around muttered.

Mike and Joseph followed the herd into the main hall and hurried upstairs. "The only good thing about this is that it's cold out," Joseph said. "Imagine if it were May instead of November and we had the windows open."

"I'm trying to imagine who made such a mess," Mike replied. "And for some dumb reason, Andy Simms' face keeps popping into my mind."

But it wasn't Andy Simms who got his shoulder tapped by Sister Mary John half an hour later, it was Mike Costa. "You're wanted, Michael. In Sister Mary Theodore's office, right away." She wore her sternest look and Mike knew he was going to get blamed for the trouble.

Sister Mary Ted looked even meaner when Mike walked into her office. "Sit down, Michael Costa."

"Yes, Sister."

"What do you think of that mess outside, Michael Costa?"

The way she kept hammering on his name sent a shiver up Mike's spine. "I think it stinks," he said. "Smells bad, I mean."

"Yes. What else?"

"I don't know. Seems like a dirty trick."

"We agree again, a very dirty trick. What I'd like to know is why a smart boy such as yourself would pull a trick like that."

"Me? I didn't do it, Sister. Honest." *What's making her blame me?* Mike wondered. He couldn't think of a way to ask without sounding rude.

"If you didn't do it, Michael Costa, then why is an empty rubbish can with *Costa Brothers* painted on the side sitting in the schoolyard? Sitting in the schoolyard with banana mess still inside, I might add?"

"Oh, geez."

"Young man, did you just swear?"

"No, Sister. Sorry, Sister. I just . . ." Mike couldn't think of what to say next. He knew, of course, exactly why their trash can had been used and who had used it. Andy Simms had sure been busy since Friday night. But Mike couldn't prove it.

"Well?" She glared at him so hard, Mike felt like his face was on fire.

"It doesn't . . . doesn't make sense," he said slowly.

"It certainly doesn't. Vandalism seldom does. I've sent for your father. You will wait right there in that chair until he arrives." With that, she swished away in her long black skirts.

With Sister gone, Mike closed his eyes. How long would it take for Pop to get there? he wondered. And then what? Would Pop beat him or believe him?

Mike wasn't sure how long he sat there, but when Pop finally did arrive, Mike felt sweaty and cold at the same time. Pop's face was red and his eyes looked like fiery black lumps of coal.

"Did you do this thing, Michael? Tell me the truth!"

So Sister had already explained. That was a bit of a relief; Mike didn't have to hear it all over again. "No, sir. I did not. I was home most of Saturday and Sunday, helping Mom keep an eye on Grandpap."

"That's true, you were." Pop turned to Sister Mary Ted. "Sister, I understand why you would suspect my boy, since you found one of our trash cans in the middle of that mess. But let me ask you something. Is my son a smart boy? Does he do well in school?"

"He gets into fights," she said.

Pop leaned forward and stared her right in the eye. "Hey, the world's a rough place. A father's job is to make sure his son can take care of himself. Especially these days. Now, I ask you again, is my son a smart kid?"

Sister wrinkled her face and looked puzzled. "Yes, Mr. Costa. When he's not quarreling, Michael is a fine student. What are you getting at?"

Mike wondered the same thing.

"I also think my son's smart, Sister. Too smart to have pulled a dumb prank like that with a Costa Brothers trash can. That's like signing his name to the mess. Unless I miss my guess, the boy's been framed."

The wrinkles on Sister's face deepened and she studied Pop first, then turned to stare at Mike. Her stare made him feel like one of those dumb goldfish from the five-and-ten-cent store swimming around naked in a little glass bowl.

"Hmmm. You may have something there, Mr. Costa. Michael, you were involved in a fight last Friday with Andrew Simms and his friends. Does this prank, as your father calls it, have anything to do with Andrew and the fight?"

Thank you, Pop, Mike thought, *for saving my bacon.*

"I don't know, Sister," he said out loud. "The first I knew about the banana mess was when I came to school this morning and saw it. I don't know who did it or why."

"But," Pop said, "since the trouble arrived in one of our trash cans, my son will of course help clean it up."

Sister beamed at Pop. "Thank you, Mr. Costa, that's an excellent idea."

First he saves my bacon, then he fries it, Mike thought. *Boy, wait till I get ahold of Simms.*

13

Dead Men

Flexing his sore shoulders, Mike trudged up Penn Avenue the next morning through a cold, steady drizzle. He'd spent hours the day before scrubbing away banana goop and now the rain came, too late to help. Joseph had helped, though, and several other guys had too.

Rather than blame anybody out loud, the teachers had asked for *volunteers* to help clean up the mess. So six or seven guys had tackled the job. And *now* it decided to rain. Mike was having a run of bad luck, he thought. And today wasn't looking much better, for again he'd caught nothing in his traps.

He walked faster, trying to shake off the gloomy

thoughts when a big black car turned up 22nd Street from Smallman. As he stood on the corner, the car lumbered to a stop, then swung onto Penn Avenue. It was more than a car, Mike realized; it was a hearse with a sign on the side that said ALLEGHENY COUNTY CORONER'S OFFICE. Before he could even swallow, a second hearse followed.

Wow! That meant somebody had died. Two somebodies. Right in the neighborhood. A couple of guys had even worse luck than he had.

It took all Mike's willpower to turn his feet up Penn Avenue toward school instead of trying to find out more, but when he reached 19th Street, Joseph was waiting for him, his eyes wide and his body bouncing. "Did you hear? Did you hear about the dead hobos?"

"I just saw two big hearses, coming from Smallman Street. Were they for a couple of hobos?" Mike asked.

"Yep. They found them in the night. Right next to the banana warehouse."

"Do the cops think they blew up the bananas?" Mike asked. "Man, if they did, they paid a big price for a measly bunch of bananas."

"Nobody knows."

"I bet they were some of Father Cox's men. What happened?"

Joseph shrugged. "Like I said, nobody knows. In the middle of the night, my pop got called out. There were two dead guys, down by the river, behind the banana warehouse. It was too dark to see much."

"How'd they find them?"

"Pop said a dog was howling. Somebody went out to hush up the dog and found the guys lying there. Dead."

"Let's go look."

"They took them away already," Joseph said.

"I know, I saw the hearses, remember? I didn't mean look at the bodies, I meant look at the place. There might be clues."

"If there are clues, my pop will find them, now that it's daylight. You want to bring your lunch sack to my house at noon today? I didn't pack a lunch on purpose, so I'll have to go home. That way if there's news . . ."

"Sure. I'll pretend I forgot." Mike jammed his salami sandwich into one jacket pocket and his apple into the other.

When they reached school, everybody was still talking about the banana mess from the day before. News about the dead bodies hadn't hit the street yet, so Joseph got to tell about them in whispers on the playground before the first bell rang. Mike stuck right next to his pal and heard the story over and over.

"Two hobos, you say? Were they murdered?" one kid asked.

"Bet it was gangsters, like on the newsreels," a tall boy said. He lined up his hands and aimed his fingers. "Bet Al Capone busted out of jail and came here with his men and they shot the guys up with tommy guns. *Rat-tat-tat-tat-tat-tat-tat.*"

"Nah, they just got themselves blown up with those bananas."

"What if they ate the bananas?" somebody said. "That would kill anybody."

"Or maybe they ate some of the Costa brothers' famous rat sausage." That came from Andy Simms in a low whisper, but plenty loud enough for Mike to hear.

Mike elbowed Simms in the side as hard as he could. Then he shoved through the knot of boys to where Joseph now stood, on the school steps, telling his story once more.

All that morning, kids looked at each other across their desks. Mike could see some kids scribbling on scraps of paper hidden under their schoolwork. Hunches or suspicions, he figured.

When lunchtime finally came, Mike followed Joseph to his house, and they hurried inside through the basement door.

"Hey, will you look at that," Joseph said. "Laundry day. We got lucky. Let's find the underwear."

Sheets and pillowcases hung from ropes near the ceiling. As Mike edged past, a cold, wet towel brushed his face and he batted it away.

"Come on, back here," Joseph whispered.

Mike found him standing near the back wall of the cellar, next to a clothesline draped with underpants, slips and brassieres. Mike couldn't help staring. Most of the time, Joseph's sisters either teased him or ignored him. But this part of having sisters was interesting, all right. Mike squinted and tried to imagine Joseph's sisters, Maureen and Kate, wearing just the stuff that was hanging from the line.

"I keep thinking I should snitch one," Joseph said, pointing to a brassiere, "and take it to school to show the guys."

The way Mike's luck had been running, he didn't think that was such a good idea. "Your mother would find out, and Sister Mary John would probably blame me," he grumbled.

"Geez, Mike. Do you think *she* wears one of these? Sister Mary John, I mean? I bet they don't allow it."

At the thought, Mike scrunched his eyes closed. It was one thing to imagine Joseph's sisters in their underwear. But a nun? "I don't know, Joseph. And I'm not sure I want to know what the Sisters wear underneath. It's too scary. Some things are better kept hidden."

"If Sister does wear one, it would be a big one," Joseph said. "She's a tank. Come on, let's go see if there's any news about the hobos."

In the kitchen, Joseph's mother was serving warmed-up stew and she ladled out a bowl for Mike, even though he'd already pulled his sandwich out and put it on the table. After snooping through the underwear in the cellar, looking Mrs. Ryan in the eye was hard, so Mike stared at the carrots in the stew.

"Pop home?" Joseph asked. "Any news?"

"He's been here and gone again," Mrs. Ryan explained. "The investigation is finished and he has to go into the station and write up the report."

"So what happened, Ma?" Joseph demanded. "Who were the guys? Did they blow up the bananas or were they killed? Were they robbed? Shot? Knifed?"

As he listened, Mike raised his head. He held his spoon so tightly he was afraid it would bend.

"They've got a lead on one man. They think his name was Cap Billy," Mrs. Ryan said. "Father Cox went down to the morgue to identify the body. The funeral will be in two days at St. Pat's. The other man's still unknown."

"Are they the ones?" Mike asked. "Do the cops think they blew up all those bananas?"

"Did the explosion kill them?" Joseph asked.

"Hardly," Mrs. Ryan said. "Both bodies only showed up last night. The police searched the whole area on Friday night and all day Saturday and found nothing. And according to your father, the men had no marks on them."

"You mean like no cuts or bruises from the blast?" Joseph asked.

"No marks at all," his mother continued. "Your father thinks it was poison. Not far from where the poor men were found, your father's partner found a pile of bloody vomit. There were stains on their clothing as well."

"Wow!" Joseph said. "So somebody poisoned the hobos and they puked up their guts, right before they died."

Bloody vomit? Had she really said that?

"No!" Mike said, dropping his spoon and jumping up from the table. "Grandpap! I gotta go home, right away. Tell Sister I was sick or something."

"But Mike—" Joseph began.

"I gotta go home," Mike repeated. "There's something scary going on. I gotta go make sure Grandpap's all right." With that, he raced out the door and up the street toward home.

When he threw open the door of his house, Mike found Grandpap sitting in the parlor and swearing at a crooner who was singing a sappy song on the radio. Then Grandpap looked up at him. "Home already? What's up? You playing hooky?"

"No. Just had to come home. I'm not feeling too good." Mike knew it was a lie, but a small one. He really hadn't felt right until he'd seen Grandpap sitting there, healthy. He made his way back to the kitchen, where Mom was scrubbing the top of the coal stove with an old rag.

"Mike! You're home early. What's wrong? Are you sick?" She dropped the rag and hurried toward him.

Mike held up both his hands. "I'm not, but I think Grandpap is. Really sick. Did you hear about the dead hobos?"

"Everybody in the Strip has heard by now," Mom said. "Tony told me when he got home from work this morning. What does that have to do with your grandpap?"

Mike told her about going to Joseph's house for lunch and what he'd learned there. "The cops think the guys were poisoned. They were vomiting blood. Just like Grandpap. Don't you see, Mom? If there's something poisoning people, Grandpap could be the next one to die."

Mom made her way to the kitchen table, where she sat down and held her hands to her cheeks. "This is serious, Mike. If you're sure you saw blood the other night . . ."

"Positive. Mom, can't you do something?"

"I don't know. If Grandpap's memory weren't failing, we could just talk with him about all this, but . . ." She let out a big sigh. "Oh, this is so hard. He forgets so much. . . ." She held her head in her hands and stared down at the tabletop for the longest time.

When she looked up, her cheeks had gone pale, but her voice was calm and steady. "I don't know exactly what we'll do, but for now, I want you to go tell your father exactly what you've told me. He can talk to the police and find out if there's any more information. Perhaps there's a medical report on those poor men."

"Right, Mom."

"In the meantime," she continued, "we'll have to keep a close watch on your grandpap. Before you head for the warehouse, go next door and ask Aunt Marie to come over. The two of us will watch over him like a pair of mother hens until your father and uncles get home. Then we can all decide what to do next."

"Sure. I'll do it, right away. But, Mom, just one thing. Will you write me a note for Sister Mary John? Will you say I got sick, so I don't get in trouble for coming home early?"

"Of course, honey," Mom said, giving Mike a quick hug. "You did the right thing coming home to tell me. Now hurry. With all the trouble that's happening in the neighborhood just now, missing a half day of school is the least of our worries."

14

Late Night

Mike hurried to the warehouse and told Pop about Grandpap being sick. He tried to talk his way into going with Pop to the police station to ask about the dead hobos, but his father sent him right back home to help Mom keep watch on Grandpap.

Watching the old man wasn't a lot of work, though, since Grandpap seemed calm, happy to listen as Mike read to him from the newspaper. By the next day the news of the hobos might make the front page, not that Mike would read that part to Grandpap. It might be too upsetting.

When Pop got home, Mike jumped up and met

him at the front door. "What did the police say? Do they know what made those hobos die?"

Pop just shook his head. "It's too soon for answers. According to the man I spoke to, it could take up to a week for the doctors to find the cause of death."

"Guess I didn't miss much, then," Mike said. Besides, if anything new turned up, he'd surely hear about it from Joseph before Pop found out, maybe even before it hit the newspapers.

He went back to reading the sports news out loud and stayed close to Grandpap, whose calm spell lasted through supper. Afterward was another story, though. The minute Pop said *doctor* an explosion hit, worse than the bananas. Just the mention of the word set off the old man's temper and he flew into a rage that went on and on. Late into the night, as Mike lay in bed trying to fall asleep, he heard Grandpap screaming and shouting at Pop and Tony and Mom.

Even after the hollering stopped and Tony had slammed out of the house for work, Mike couldn't fall asleep. He was still awake at midnight. He heard the trains blowing their whistles, then the slow chuffing of wheels and the screech of metal on metal as the brakemen brought the engines to a stop.

He climbed out of bed and threw open his back window. Maybe he should go down to Smallman Street and help the uncles haul crates, he thought, breathing in the cold night air. Maybe if he worked for a couple of hours he'd get tired enough to sleep.

Mike eased on his clothes, making sure not to step on the loose floorboard near the end of his bed. If he woke Mom and Pop, he'd have a tough time explaining why he was up and dressed at this hour. Moving silently, like one of those sneaky rats he was supposed to catch, he made his way from the attic to the second floor, and at last to the front hall. Mom and Pop's bedroom was upstairs in the back of the house, so if he crept out the front door they wouldn't wake up.

He carefully unlocked the door and pushed it open and then he was free—outside at night, breathing in the cold air and watching the streetlights shine in the dark. Beyond his block he could hear the hum of the men who worked all night, and he turned toward the sound, ready to join them. He knew Tony wouldn't tell on him, and he hoped Roberto wouldn't either.

He hesitated on the sidewalk for a moment, still deciding whether to go. Once outside, he didn't have to sneak around anymore, but something jangled his nerves. What was it? *Probably too quiet here,* he thought. *I'll feel fine when I get over to Smallman Street and all the hustle-bustle.*

Mike turned up the side street toward Smallman and the river. He took long steps, hurrying to leave the quiet behind. He'd covered most of the block when a large shape appeared out of the darkness, silhouetted by the streetlight at the corner. The shape—it looked like a man—was moving.

Mike stopped dead to watch. Only his heart

seemed alive, but it was kicking up so much fuss he wondered if the man could hear it.

Odd thing, though, he realized after a moment. The man, if that's what it was, wasn't moving toward him. Instead it seemed to be rocking back and forth, swaying and bumping its head into the edge of somebody's fence. Why would a person do such a thing? Mike wondered.

He took a couple of steps closer and heard muttering. "Where's the gate? Dang gate, where's that gate?" Mike's breath caught. It sounded like—it was—Grandpap.

"No," Mike blurted out. "Grandpap! What are you doing?" He rushed toward the old man and grabbed hold of his arm. "Come on, stop bumping that fence."

"What? Who are you? What do you want with me?" He pulled and tried to twist away.

"It's me, Mike. I'm your grandson, Vincent's son. Come on, Grandpap, it's late. You need to be in bed."

"But I work nights. I work down on Smallman, unloading the trains," Grandpap said. "Don't I?" He stopped struggling and looked down at himself.

Then Mike noticed that Grandpap was barefoot, wearing his pajamas. "Tonight's your night off," Mike said. "Tony and Roberto are covering the job right now. Come on, it's cold and dark out here. You need to come back inside."

Gently, he tugged on Grandpap's arm, half pulling, half leading him back to Penn Avenue. When they reached their house, Mike didn't worry about noise. He shoved open the door, helped Grandpap inside and slammed the door on purpose so Mom and Pop would wake up and come down.

It didn't take more than a minute for them to appear, first Pop and then Mom, tying the belt of her robe as she came downstairs.

"Pop! Michael! What's going on?" Pop hurried over and put his hands on Grandpap's shoulders.

"I . . . I heard a noise," Mike said, making up the best lie he could on short notice. "And . . . and when I looked out the window, I saw somebody. I thought it might be Grandpap, so I threw on my clothes to go check. . . ."

"Thank heavens you did," Mom said, pulling him into a warm, comforting hug. "And now let's get you both back to bed."

15

The CCC

The next morning heavy rain was pelting the Strip again when Mike finally dragged himself down to the kitchen. "Cheer up, son," Pop said after breakfast as they unfurled umbrellas and started out the door. "These storms have washed away those stinking bananas at long last."

"Amen," Uncle Frank said in a loud, cheery voice as he joined them.

As they walked, Pop and Uncle Frank talked about Grandpap. Mike wished he could close up his ears and shut out the words. It wasn't that his family didn't care about the old man; they just didn't seem to know how to make him see a doctor to figure out what was causing the sick spells.

"You haven't caught many rats lately, have you, Mike?" Pop asked when they reached the warehouse and hurried inside.

Mike stamped his feet, shaking off the rain that had splashed under the umbrella. "Nope. I think they've been eating bananas. Now that it's raining, they'll probably come back inside. I sure would."

"Smart boy," Uncle Frank teased. "You catch some big ones, now. I hear tell there's a spare nickel with your name on it in the cash register. Wouldn't want to make a nickel sit there and wait, would you?"

Mike grinned. "No, sir." He kept grinning all the way down the steps to the cellar. If Uncle Frank was talking about spare nickels, then maybe the business wasn't in such terrible shape after all. And he could have ice cream.

The rats didn't cooperate. As on the two previous days, the first two traps he checked were empty. He kicked the cellar wall, then studied the traps and tried to think of a way to arrange them better. Tony had told him to put them along the walls, because that was where those lousy rats liked to run. Mike nudged a trap out a foot or two from the corner and then noticed that it had been sprung. Again.

"Darn sneak." Quickly, he checked the other traps and found three more that had been sprung. "You're springing all the traps and eating all the bait; no wonder I can't catch anything. Well, I'll fix you, just you wait."

Carefully, he bumped each remaining trap with the toe of his shoe, springing them open with loud snaps. Then he collected them all in his bucket and reset them with bigger hunks of cheese rind. After arranging the traps the best way he knew, he trudged back up the stairs.

"You won't talk me out of this, Franco," Tony was saying as Mike opened the door.

Mike was tempted to slink partway back down the stairs and eavesdrop, but he decided not to. Instead he walked quietly into the front room of the warehouse, where the four Costa brothers had gathered. He'd listen, but he wouldn't hide.

"If it's because of last night," Pop began, "you know as well as I do the old man isn't usually that rough."

"I signed up yesterday morning. Hours before the old man blew up."

Signed up? For what? Mike eased closer to the circle of men. Nobody seemed to notice.

"I still don't understand," Uncle Frank complained. "We're a family. This is a family business. How can you just up and leave?"

"I can handle his work." Roberto spoke slowly and carefully. "It's not like Tony's leaving us in the lurch."

Mike frowned. It sounded like Roberto was in on this, whatever it was.

"But it will be hard on you, Roberto—" Pop began.

"No, it won't," Tony interrupted. "You want the truth, there isn't enough work for two night men. And that was before Sal lost his store."

"But the CCC, that's like going on relief. No brother of mine goes on relief." Uncle Frank's face was red and his voice was loud.

Going on relief? The words sent a rush of shame over Mike. His fingernails dug into his palms. Going on relief meant taking money from the government, something Tony should never need to do; at least, Mike hoped not.

"It's not relief. It's work, hard work. Building things. Look, I know we got a family business," Tony said. "But nobody ever asked me if I liked the business. Maybe I don't want to sell salami for the rest of my life. I'm the youngest, so everybody just acts like I have to go along. But I'm a man now. I can make my own choices."

Wow, you tell him, Tony. Although Mike had always planned to work with Pop and the uncles, it was only fair for Tony to choose his own life.

Uncle Frank glared. "So you're going to work for the government down in West Virginia making some kind of crazy Boy Scout camp? It don't make sense, Tony!" He thumped his fist against the counter.

"Now, hold on, Franco," Pop said.

His voice sounded sensible; at least Mike thought so. Good thing Pop ran the business instead of Uncle Frank.

Pop turned to Tony. "If you don't want to sell salami, what do you want to do?"

"I like making things. Building things. The Civilian Conservation Corps does that. Takes young guys like me and gives them a chance to learn to build—cabins, lodges, roads, trails. It's a big state park, not some puny little scout camp, Franco."

"He'll be good," Roberto said. "Look at that fence he built out behind our houses. Still standing and straight as the day he set the posts."

Tony shot a grin at Roberto. "That's right, I will be good. And it makes things easier for the family too. You won't have me to feed, and the squirt here," he said, pointing at Mike, "the squirt can move downstairs from the attic."

Everybody turned and seemed to notice Mike at the same time, but nobody scolded him for being there. He scuffed one toe on the floor.

"The best part is," Tony went on, "it's a real job. I get paid. The CCC provides me with food, clothes, tools and a place to stay, and they send my wages home to the family, so I'll be helping out. Come on, Vincent, sign the papers." He passed an envelope to Pop.

Mike's fingers itched to see what was inside.

"You don't cost that much to feed," Uncle Frank grumbled. "And you ain't twenty-one yet, so we don't have to let you go."

"In three months I will be. Then I can do what I want," Tony said. "Please, Vincent."

Mike turned and studied his father's face. *Please don't sign it,* he wanted to say. *He's the closest thing I've got to a brother, so don't let him go down to West Virginia.* But Mike held his tongue. Truth was, he didn't blame Tony for wanting to go off and have an adventure. If Mike had been old enough, he'd have tagged along. Shoot, maybe he could stow away in one of Tony's duffel bags.

"You sure about this, Anthony?" Pop asked.

"Positive."

Pop lifted the flap on the envelope and pulled out the papers. "All right, I'll sign. But we aren't spending your money. We'll save it up so when you come home, you'll have a nest egg. No arguments about that."

Good for you, Pop. Mike grinned in spite of himself.

Tony shrugged. He elbowed Roberto and they headed out the door.

"You'll be sorry, Vincent," Uncle Frank warned.

"I already am sorry," Pop answered. "But not because Tony wants to spread his wings. I'm just sorry because I'll miss him." He reached out and caught Mike's neck in a headlock and hugged him roughly. "So, Michael Costa, you man enough to take on some of your uncle's chores at home once he goes to work for the dang government?"

"Sure, Pop. Sure." Mike stood tall and puffed out his chest, but it was hard. He'd miss Tony worse than Pop would. *Dang government,* he thought, sounding in his mind as tough as Uncle Frank. *Dang government and hard times are busting up everything, even Costa Brothers.*

16

No Recess

At the corner of 19th Street, Joseph was waiting for Mike with a worried frown. "Hey, what took you so long? We gotta hustle if we're going to make it to school on time."

"Sorry. I spent extra time at the warehouse this morning. . . ."

"You catch a lot of rats, then? Got full pockets?"

"Nope. Empty traps again. How about you?"

Joseph jingled the coins in his pocket. "I'm a millionaire. Hey, maybe the reason you didn't catch any is because they all came to my street to die. Pop paid me a nickel to shovel four dead rats from the backyard into the trash. Then old Mrs. Larkin next door saw some in her backyard and she paid me another nickel, so I got ten cents to spend. I can treat you to ice cream today. Or we could get a big milk shake and split it."

Mike didn't want to be a charity case, but it had been a while since he'd stopped by Klavon's. Besides, you shouldn't act proud with friends. "Maybe. I'll think about it." He frowned.

"Geez, Mike, what's the matter now?"

"Tony. He's leaving town." Mike went on to explain about the CCC. "That's why I was late today. Sorry."

"Tough news," Joseph said. "I'd hate it if one of my brothers went off like that." He turned, grinned and poked Mike in the side. "But you could take both my sisters and I wouldn't mind at all. West Virginia might not be far enough for them. You should have heard the screeching this morning when they saw those dead rats. You'd have thought the rats were on the kitchen table instead of in the backyard."

At the mention of Joseph's sisters, Mike remembered their underwear and felt his cheeks go hot. Hoping his friend wouldn't notice, he looked down at the sidewalk as they crossed 15th Street. There, in the gutter, lay a pair of dead rats, heads twisted to one side as if they'd died in pain.

"Look at that. More rats." Mike pointed with the toe of his shoe. "Wish the darn things would die in my traps instead of on the streets. Wonder what's going on?"

"Bet they got sick from eating too much banana cream pie."

Mike waved his hand in front of his face. "Phew. Glad it rained. I've about had it with rotten bananas."

"*We're* going to be the rotten bananas if we're late. Come on," Joseph said. "And think about splitting a milk shake after school."

"Okay. I will." Mike hustled inside the school and upstairs in record time, barely beating the bell. But when he'd opened his reader, he couldn't pay attention to the words on the pages. He noticed Andy Simms in the next row grinning and drawing more rat pictures, but for some reason he couldn't be bothered with Simms. He wasn't thinking about milk shakes either, but about Tony leaving. They hadn't said exactly when he would go, but from the way Pop and the uncles had been talking, it sounded like soon. And Mike would get Tony's room.

He shook his head. He didn't want the dumb room. He liked his attic just fine, liked the way the ceiling slanted down on the sides, and the way a window fitted into each end, letting in cool breezes on hot nights. Besides, if he took over Tony's room, then his uncle wouldn't have a place to come home to when the CCC job finished. Sure, he could stay with Uncle Frank, but Mike liked having him in the same house. He liked having somebody else around when Grandpap slipped into one of his moods. *Grandpap.*

A shadow fell over Mike's shoulder. From behind he could hear the rustle of Sister Mary John's long black skirts. "Michael Costa, what are you doing this morning? You haven't turned a page in fifteen minutes."

"Sorry, Sister. I—"

"You'll see me at recess," she said with a stern look.

Mike hid his tightened fists under his desk. *Darn Sister anyway.* Joseph was right, she looked like a tank and acted like a general. Just once he'd like to poke his foot out into the aisle and maybe trip her, but you couldn't do that to nuns; they had some sort of holy protection, Joseph said. If you bothered them, your sins piled up. You probably shouldn't think about their underwear either, Mike decided.

He turned his attention back to the reader and tried to finish the story, but he kept thinking of Grandpap and how sick he'd been. And those dead hobos. He could imagine it all—two dirty, unshaven men, wearing just thin, worn overcoats, lying on their sides, all curled up like their stomachs hurt. Except that when Mike imagined the dead hobos, their faces looked like Grandpap's. What if the same thing that had killed the hobos was making Grandpap sick? How could a person find out?

Mike lowered his eyes and forced himself to read three paragraphs so he could turn the page for Sister. Then he glanced over at Simms' artwork again and it hit him. The dead rats!

All the dead rats he'd seen on the street had looked rotten. Some had bloated stomachs. So maybe, just maybe, whatever had killed the hobos was also killing the rats. Maybe they'd died from something other than eating rotten bananas. Something worse. And Grandpap? Was he next?

Mike could barely wait to talk it over with Joseph, but when recess came and the other kids raced outside, he still sat at his desk, facing Sister Mary John.

"Michael, you've been far away this morning. And during the past few days, your behavior and grades haven't been at all acceptable. Does this have something to do with last week's fight? Or the banana mess?"

"No, Sister, it's . . ." He didn't want to explain about Tony. If he did, it might sound like he was telling about Costa Brothers and how the business was having trouble. And he didn't think she'd like hearing about dead rats any more than Joseph's sisters had liked seeing them.

He took a deep breath and sighed. "It's my grandpap. He's been sick and he won't go to the doctor."

Sister Mary John's square face softened. "I'm sorry to hear that, Michael. You should have told me sooner. I'd have made allowances. . . ." She straightened again. "You still need to get your work done, but I do understand if you have things on your mind. Now, let's see how many pages you can complete before your classmates return from recess."

"Yes, Sister." Mike bent his head down and stared at the reader so she couldn't see him frown. Now he'd have to wait until after school to talk to Joseph. But he'd better get some work done and fast, or else she'd make him stay after school too.

17

Cap Billy

"I'd say you need that milk shake more than ever," Joseph said that afternoon as they left school and made their way down Penn Avenue. "How bad did she holler?"

"So-so. She says I have to work harder. No more goofing off. Did I miss anything at recess?"

"Boy, did you ever. Simms must have spent all morning drawing pictures of rats."

Fire rose from Mike's belly and made his cheeks grow hot. "And?"

"He put your name on them. Was passing them out to everybody. I grabbed as many as I could." Joseph reached into his pocket, pulled out five wrinkled sheets of paper and handed them to Mike one by one.

Mike took his time, studying the pages. In each one a rat sat in the center of the page with an evil snarl on its face. Underneath, just one word—*COSTA*. Simms had taken his time, on both the drawings and the writing, for the drawings looked real enough to bite and the script was dark, large and fancied up.

Mike balled up the papers and stuffed them into his coat pockets, then grabbed Joseph by one arm and glared in his friend's face. "He's a dirty rat. I've got to do something. Will you help?"

"Hey, it's Simms you're mad at, not me," Joseph said, pulling his arm free. "I'm in, but we'd better wait till tomorrow so we can figure out a good plan. And you're right, Mike, he is a rat."

Rats. Mike shook his head, trying to clear away all thoughts of that lousy Simms. He had important things on his mind. "Look, Joseph. I got an idea this morning. Remember at Klavon's when my grandpap came in? He's been having stomach trouble for a while and I started wondering. What if something—a poison, like your pop said—what if it's killing rats and those hobos and making my grandpap sick?"

"Bananas?"

"Not bananas. Grandpap got sick before the explosion. Something else."

"Could be," Joseph said. "It's a good idea. But how can you find out?"

"This afternoon, while I was drawing that map and filling in all the states, I got to thinking. What gives you a stomachache? What makes you throw up? It's usually something you ate, right?"

"Yeah, ate or drank. When I was three, I drank a whole jar of pickle juice. Boy, was that nasty." Joseph rubbed his stomach.

Mike had to laugh. "How could you drink a whole jar of pickle juice?"

"Sweet pickles, Mike. I love 'em. But now I leave the juice behind. I learned the hard way, I'm no dummy."

"See, that's the trouble exactly," Mike said. "Let's say the rats are eating something that kills them off, but face it, they're kinda dumb. They can't talk to tell what they ate."

"They're also dead," Joseph added. "And so are the hobos, so they can't talk either. Which leaves your grandpap."

"I know," Mike said. "And Grandpap doesn't remember things. I mean, sure, he can tell all about a fight he had fifty years ago when he was a kid, but by noon he doesn't remember what happened that morning. So what do we do? I've been thinking and thinking and nothing comes."

"Hold on," Joseph said. "We do know some. If you're right, if people and rats are getting sick from eating or drinking the same bad stuff, we could figure out what people and rats could both get hold of. We also know that it's happening right here, in the Strip. So we can snoop around."

"Yeah, I like the sound of that," Mike agreed. "Finding hidden stuff, sorta like private eyes."

Joseph stopped short and pointed with his right thumb up 17th Street toward Liberty Avenue. "Father Cox's church is just over there. We could stop by. Ask Father what he knows about the dead hobos."

Mike stared up the street in the direction of the church. Talking with Father Cox would mean crossing through that shantytown, passing by all those dirty, hungry men. But this was for Grandpap, so Mike couldn't be a yellow belly.

"Yeah. Okay, let's do it, right now." *Before I lose my nerve,* he thought.

Joseph led the way up 17th Street toward the church and Mike let him. If anything, he wished Joseph were taller, so he could slip along behind, hidden in his friend's shadow. He'd rather fight Andy Simms and his three mean pals again than get close to the shantytown hobos.

In the churchyard at the corner of Liberty Avenue men huddled around fires they'd built from busted-up old crates. Smoke billowed in the air and Mike caught the scent of unwashed bodies. He shuddered.

Hurrying between the gates behind Joseph, he tried not to look into any of the faces. It seemed like a mile to the church door, but once inside, he glanced around. A few older women knelt in front of the Blessed Virgin.

106

The boys kept walking, quietly, toward one side of the church where a door led behind the altar. Joseph, who was an altar boy and knew his way around, knocked on the door. "Father Cox. Are you there, Father?"

The door opened and the priest stepped out. He had dark hair and a friendly smile. "Well, Joseph Ryan. And Michael Costa. Welcome to St. Pat's." He waved his hand in the general direction of the confessionals. "It's not Saturday yet; are your sins so weighty that you need to make an early confession?"

Mike wondered if they'd have to tell about the snooping they'd done in Joseph's basement the day before. Telling that to a priest would be embarrassing.

Joseph shook his head. "No thanks, Father. We already confessed last week's fight. We came about the hobos who died."

"I've already told the police what I know," the priest said. "One guy they called Cap Billy, the other one I hadn't seen before."

"The one you knew, had he been sick?" Mike asked, focusing his attention on the reason for their visit.

"I don't know. What are you getting at, boys?"

"Just wondering is all," Joseph said. "Wish we could find out more."

Father Cox tilted his head to one side. "There is somebody you could ask. A fellow outside was a friend of Billy's. He might know something. Come on, I'll introduce you."

The priest stepped briskly down the aisle. Joseph

fell in behind him, but Mike stood still for a minute. If he'd heard right, he and Joseph were going to have to talk to one of those hobos. That seemed like a terrible idea.

The priest glanced back over his shoulder at Mike. It felt like the man was staring right into Mike's soul and could see the bad thoughts, see what a coward he was. Father Cox gave him a quick nod and turned back toward the church door.

Ashamed, Mike hustled to catch up. He had to do this for Grandpap, so he wouldn't get sick again. And for Father Cox, so the priest wouldn't think he was chicken-livered.

18

In Shantytown

Out in the shantytown, Father Cox moved among the men, smiling and shaking hands or touching their shoulders lightly. He didn't seem to care that they wore filthy clothes and smelled like sweat. Mike tried not to think about that and kept walking.

In a far corner the priest stopped and squatted next to a small, smoking fire. A thin man with a gray beard and gray hair poking out around the edges of a knitted cap was tending the fire. "Good day to you, Pete. I got a couple of young fellows here. They'd like to talk with you about Cap Billy. Do you have the time?"

"Oh, Father, I got nothing but time."

As Father Cox stood and headed back toward the church, the hobo turned to the boys with a grin that showed yellowed teeth. "Pull up a *sit*, and *chair* down." He pointed to the dirt and Joseph squatted as the priest had.

Mike joined him and opened his mouth to begin asking questions, but his voice didn't seem to work. All he could do was stare at the raggedy edges of the man's coat sleeve.

"We were wondering," Joseph began. "Father Cox says you were a friend of Cap Billy's."

"Sure was. He and a couple others shared this corner with me." The man waved toward a shack made of scraps of lumber, crates and rusting tin. "Home sweet home. What you want to know?"

Mike cleared his throat. "The man—Cap Billy—had he been sick? Complaining of stomach pains?" His voice sounded rough, like he had knots tied in his tongue, but at least he'd gotten it working again. The sooner they found answers, the sooner they could leave, he decided.

The hobo named Pete shook his head sadly. "Ain't a man here who don't complain of stomach pains, boys. You know what hunger feels like?"

The question felt like an accusation and Mike wanted to disappear. Instead, he swallowed hard and shook his head. Joseph did the same.

"You're lucky, then, and don't you forget it. Hard to know about Billy, though. Maybe he was sick, maybe he just got weak, maybe some fever came and carried him off."

"We're real sorry you lost a friend," Joseph said. "What was he like?"

Mike looked at his friend in amazement. Probably it came from being a cop's son, but Joseph seemed to know how to talk to this man and how to ask his questions in a nice way, so they might get answers.

"He was a corker," the hobo said. "Knew more swear words than any five other guys. Claimed he worked the tugs from the time he was a boy, and I believed it. That's how he got to be called Cap, short for Captain."

"Did he spend a lot of time down by the water?" Joseph asked.

"Sure did. He was a river man. He'd even go down there at night and just watch the water flow by. Sometimes he'd squint, like he was trying to see faraway places— maybe places he'd been to or where he'd come from. But he's in a different place now. Better place too, if the Lord don't hold it against him for all that swearing."

"Did your friend . . . ," Mike began. "Did Cap Billy eat or drink anything that might have made him sick?"

"Shoot, sonny boy, didn't you hear me before? Down here, you eat what you can, what you find. And you don't look too close. Sure, sometimes you might get something that's a little off, but if you're lucky, your stomach toughens up. Billy, he wasn't lucky, and that's the plain truth of it."

"Thank you, sir," Joseph said. "We appreciate you telling us what you know."

"Yes, sir," Mike added. "Thank you." He scrambled to his feet.

The man stood as well and stuck out his hand. Joseph shook it and then Mike did too, suddenly ashamed that he hadn't been the first to shake. The hobo might be dirty and rough, but he'd been nice to them. And they'd come here to help Mike's grandpap, not Joseph's, so he should have been friendlier.

"Take care, now, boys," the man said. "Hope you find what you're looking for."

"Thanks," Mike said again, giving the man a quick wave before turning and following Joseph up the walk and out the gates.

When they reached Penn Avenue, Mike let out a big sigh. "That was a waste of time. We don't know much more than we did before."

"Wish he'd told us something big," Joseph agreed. "But now we know those men will eat spoiled food. Cap Billy probably did."

"Rats will do that too," Mike said.

"What about your grandpap?" Joseph asked carefully. "Could he get mixed up enough to eat something that was rotting?"

Mike shrugged. "Maybe. Mom says he sometimes forgets if he's had lunch and eats twice. So sure, he might pick up a rotten apple or some moldy bread. Shoot, some days he's so bad, he might even drink river water for all I know."

"Nobody drinks river water," Joseph said.

"I know," Mike said. "I was just saying he might."

As Joseph stopped and stared at Mike, a thoughtful

frown crossed his face. "If he did drink some . . . Hey, you might have something there," he said. "Between the sewers and the factories, that river water's rotten. But I bet rats drink it. Hobos might too; heck, I've seen them shave in it. So if your grandpap was out fishing and got thirsty enough . . ."

"Yeah, he might forget how lousy the water is and drink some." Just saying the words made Mike's mouth pucker. He'd been warned about that water so many times he doubted he'd be able to swallow a single mouthful in the middle of a drought. But Grandpap, the way his brain worked these days, he could do just about anything. And maybe he had.

"Hey, Mike, let's split an Allegheny River float at Klavon's." Joseph elbowed him in the ribs and grinned.

Mike shook his head. Even though he knew an Allegheny River float was just Coca-Cola with vanilla ice cream dumped in, the thought of a river-water float gave him the heebie-jeebies.

"No thanks," he told Joseph. "I'll skip Klavon's today. We spent a lot of time talking to that guy in the churchyard. Don't want to be late for supper or Mom will holler." As he walked down Penn Avenue toward home, the lie tasted bad in Mike's mouth, but not nearly as bad as river water.

19

Old Sneaky

Mike was still stewing about the river water the next morning as he followed his father and uncle to the warehouse. Best he could figure, somebody would have to drink a bunch of it, then wait and see if he got sick. Sounded like a pretty dangerous mission—so dangerous that even Jack Armstrong, the All-American Boy, might turn it down.

Mike didn't feel like playing hero. He rubbed his belly. Just the thought of drinking river water made his stomach jump around. Still, somebody had to be the guinea pig.

Once at the warehouse, Pop and Uncle Frank hurried out to the loading dock as usual, leaving Mike inside to take care of his traps. The minute he opened the cellar door, he heard loud squeals and knew he'd caught a live one, which didn't improve the condition of his stomach.

Yanking his gloves on, he picked up the pail. As he flipped on the cellar light and started downstairs, the squeals grew louder, so he hurried, following the noise to a back corner by the furnace. Sure enough, a live rat had one bloody front paw stuck fast under the trap's bar. It had fought the trap, though, and dragged it away from the wall.

Mike swallowed hard. Even as he stood there, the rat snapped, snarled and tried to pull away, but the trap was too strong. Mike set down his bucket and went to find a sturdy board near where he kept his chopping knife. With a two-by-four in hand, he returned to the rat. One stiff whack was all it would take, and the sooner the better. "This will teach you to mess with my traps, you greedy beast," he said.

Mike raised the board and began to swing it toward the snapping, snarling rat. Then he stopped and let the board slip to the floor.

"Greedy," he repeated. "I wonder . . . Are you thirsty too? If you are, you can be the guinea pig and I won't have to drink a single drop of that river water."

Picking up the rat by the tail, he flung it, trap and all, into his bucket. The rat screeched, and scrabbled against the pail. Mike held it at arm's length and raced to the far corner of the cellar, where Pop stacked all his old empty containers. Sure enough, Mike spotted an oversized glass pickle jar with a screw-on lid. It looked as big as a toilet bowl, but pretty clean, so he unscrewed the lid and set the jar next to the bucket.

The hard part came next. Mike bit down on his bottom lip and tried to steady his hands. Quickly, he dumped out the rat and trap, and set the heavy glass jar upside down over most of the rat's struggling body so only the trap and the captured front leg poked out. Then, setting his knee on the jar to keep it from moving, he bent and carefully unsprang the trap.

Lightning fast, the rat pulled its sore leg inside and began to lick it. While the rat was busy with the leg, Mike held his breath, tipped the jar on one side and heaved the rat in farther with his gloved hand. Then he jammed the lid on and screwed it down tight. With a sigh of relief, he set the jar upright. The rat clawed the jar and tried to scratch at him through the glass.

Now all he had to do was poke a couple of holes in the lid and drop in enough cheese to keep the rat happy until school let out. And if he put some salt on that cheese, Old Sneaky would build up a thirst, so the rat would drink a hefty dose of that foul river water.

By the time Mike finished with the holes and checked and reset the rest of his traps, his hands had stopped trembling. He'd be late for school and probably miss recess again, but it was for a good cause. After school, he and Joseph could stop by the warehouse and fix up a container of river water for Old Sneaky to drink. Then all they'd have to do was watch and wait.

Mike didn't have to wait long to find out that he was in trouble. Sister Mary John glared at him when he tried to ease into the classroom and take his seat.

Simms must have caught the glare, for he turned to Mike with a wicked grin. "In trouble again, Rat Boy? Where were you, helping your pop make some of that sausage? Or maybe you were sampling some." Simms licked his lips and whispered softly, but in Mike's mind the words rang as loudly as the school bell.

He gave Simms' desk a quick shove that sent three books to the floor. "Later, you bum," he promised. But it couldn't be that afternoon, he realized. That afternoon, he had to try to poison a real rat. Maybe if it worked, he'd figure out a way to make Simms drink river water. Wouldn't that be something?

Once school let out, Mike and Joseph hightailed it down to the Allegheny's edge. Mike explained his plan as they went.

"Salty cheese and river water, that's smart, Mike."

"Hope it works." A cold, damp wind rose up from the slate gray water, but at least it didn't stink. In the summer the river smelled foul, but today the cold, windy weather seemed to blow away the worst of the stench.

After crossing the train tracks, they poked around in a pile of trash that lay between the tracks and the river. Mike held up a root beer bottle. "We can carry water in this. Now we need something small for the rat to drink from."

"How about this?" Joseph asked, showing Mike a tin can.

"Too tall. Half that big would be better."

Joseph kicked aside a bunch of dried weeds and dug up a smaller can, one that had probably held tuna fish.

"Perfect."

Squatting, Mike swished cold cloudy water around in the bottle, then the tin can. Shaking the can to dry it, he passed it to Joseph, then leaned over and filled the root beer bottle to the top.

With his thumb over the bottle's opening to keep the water from spilling, Mike hurried along the tracks toward 22nd Street and the warehouse.

Joseph loped alongside. "Sure can't wait to see that rat you caught."

"Old Sneaky," Mike said. "I know he's been stealing my bait."

When they arrived at the warehouse, Mike hid the root beer bottle inside his coat. "Hi, Pop, came to check the traps again. I'm getting pretty hungry for ice cream."

"Tell you what, boys, even if you don't catch anything, I'll treat you to a cone each." Pop reached into the cash register and flipped Mike a pair of nickels.

"Thanks, Pop."

"Yeah, thanks, Mr. Costa," Joseph echoed.

Mike led the way down the cellar stairs. At the bottom, he paused for a moment and listened. No squealing or squeaking. He wondered what that meant. Hurrying to the back corner, he set down the bottle of water and moved the wooden crates he'd used to hide Old Sneaky's jar. When he pulled the jar out, the rat in the bottom lay suspiciously quiet, a solid grayish lump.

Joseph peered into the jar. "Darn, looks like he's a goner."

"Maybe he's just sleeping," Mike said. "Rats are like that, they run around more at night." He shook the jar and Old Sneaky moved a little.

"You said you gave him a lot of salt with the cheese this morning," Joseph began. "Think he might be thirsty? Too thirsty to do anything but lie around?"

"I hope so. It's not so bad if he's conked out when we put the tin can in the jar." He passed the jar to Joseph. "Here, hold this for a minute while I go get the gloves."

"I'll help," Joseph said when Mike returned. "Give me a glove and I'll block the top of the jar while you reach in with the tin can."

Joseph set the jar on an upside-down crate. Mike put on the right glove and passed his friend the left one. Then, with his ungloved hand, he gently twisted the metal jar lid until it was nearly off. "You ready? I want to get this over with."

"Ready." Joseph pulled on the left glove and slipped the lid from the jar, quickly covering the top with the glove.

Heart pounding, Mike picked up the old tuna can and nodded. "Give me a little room."

Joseph slipped his hand to one side and Mike shoved the tin can in, keeping hold of it until it touched the bottom of the jar. That seemed to rouse the rat, which bared its teeth and snapped at the glove.

Mike yanked his hand out, leaving the glove behind. Then, carefully, he poked two fingers back into the jar and grabbed the glove. He had to shake it to free the thumb from the darn rat's teeth, but at least the critter wasn't dead.

Once Mike had slipped the glove out of the jar, Joseph quickly screwed down the lid. Inside the jar, the rat bared its teeth and clawed at the glass with its uninjured front paw. "Whew, we did it," Joseph said. "He's a hot one, isn't he?"

"Yeah, water might cool him off." Mike picked up the root beer bottle and tipped it gently over one of the holes. He kept pouring until the tin was full. Still the rat arched its back and attacked the glass jar.

"Bottoms up, Old Sneaky," Joseph said. "Come on, drink, you dummy. Aren't you thirsty?" He turned to Mike. "We got a couple nickels, how about an Allegheny River float at Klavon's? In honor of this old rat."

Today, knowing he wouldn't have to drink any real river water, Mike could laugh at the idea. "I'm thirsty all right, but I'd vote for a chocolate milk shake made with chocolate ice cream."

"What about him?" Joseph asked, pointing at the jar, where Old Sneaky had finally stopped fighting and was poking his snout into the water.

"I'll hide him behind some crates again so Pop won't find him."

"And tomorrow? Will you give him more salty cheese and river water?"

"If I need to, but if we're lucky, by tomorrow he'll be dead."

20

A Noisy Desk

The next morning Joseph was standing on the corner of 19th Street when Mike arrived. "Did he die? Did Old Sneaky kick the bucket?"

"Not yet," Mike grumbled.

"Did he throw up? Did you see any blood, Mike?"

"Nothing. He looks better than yesterday. His front leg seems to be healing and he only snapped a little. He ate the cheese rind I dropped in and licked up the salt too."

"How about the river water? Did he drink it all?"

"Every drop. I filled the tin can again this morning, but if he isn't dead by afternoon . . ."

"Maybe it isn't river water after all," Joseph finished.

"I was so sure he would die in the night," Mike grumbled. "How could anybody drink that filthy water and not get sick?"

Joseph shrugged. "Rats are pretty tough. They live in the sewers, after all. Maybe they like that rotten stuff."

Mike shook his head. Rats were really disgusting. Even talking about that water made his stomach twist. At 17th Street he glanced up toward Father Cox's church. "Geez, if it isn't river water, what else could it be? What could rats, hobos and my grandpap all get hold of?"

"I know," Joseph said. He lowered his voice to a whisper. "It's got to be something they ate or drank; we figured that out already, right?"

"So?"

"So my pop is always warning my brothers to stay away from hooch—you know, moonshine."

Everybody knew about moonshine and hooch, Mike thought. How could you not know, living beside the river? Sure, making, buying and selling liquor was against the law these days, but not everybody obeyed the law. And in Pittsburgh, with three big rivers, boats could drift along at night when nobody could see and smugglers could unload their illegal cargoes. Mike hadn't seen it happen, but Tony and Roberto had, more than once.

"Pop says the stuff Old Bertucci sells is good clean booze, smuggled in from Canada," Joseph continued. He poked his thumb to the right toward the river. "But some guy with a still could make a rotten batch. Pop's seen guys in the drunk tank who got real sick from bad hooch. Would your grandpap drink moonshine?"

"Probably," Mike said. "And hobos might too."

Joseph nodded. "Exactly. And if some bad hooch spilled or got dumped out, the rats would find it. They go after anything. So if the river water doesn't work, let's try moonshine next."

As they neared the steps of St. Patrick's School, Mike lowered his voice too. "Only one problem, Joseph. Where are *we* going to get moonshine?"

"I don't know, but I bet my brothers do. I'll talk to them tonight, and on Saturday we'll go find us a moonshiner and some hooch. Peachy, huh?"

Mike swallowed. It was for Grandpap, he reminded himself. Joseph's pop was a cop, so he'd help them out if they got caught. He nodded and tried to smile as they pushed open the school door. "Yeah, Joseph. Peachy."

When they got to class, though, it was anything but peachy for Mike. When he took his seat, he laid his schoolbooks on top of his desk. A high-pitched squeak sounded. The girl who sat behind him started to giggle, making Mike scowl.

With light, careful fingers, he lifted his books off the desk, one at a time, and set them in his lap. That didn't make any noise, so he lifted the top of the desk and set the books inside. Still quiet, so whatever had happened must have been an accident.

When Sister strode in, the class stood to greet her and said their morning prayers. As Mike sat down, he leaned on the desk and again heard a loud squeak, which made him jump back.

Next to him, Simms grinned and echoed the sound. "*Squeak, squeak.* Talk to us, Rat Boy."

"I should have known," Mike muttered, trying to peer underneath his desk. All he could see was the heavy metal base, but it didn't look any different from the other kids' desks.

He spent the morning acting like his desk was made of eggshells. He didn't slam it, didn't even lean on it hard, yet still the squeaking came, like a live animal was hiding inside. The noise seemed to be worse on the right side. He lifted the lid but saw no sign of motion, nothing that didn't belong, only papers, books, pencils and a couple of good-luck stones. They'd sure let him down.

He crossed his fingers and hoped the noise was too far away for Sister to hear, but the kids around him heard it. And after the second time, they giggled, covered their mouths and squeaked back, even the girls. A little before lunch, after what must have been the tenth or twentieth squeak, he dropped his pencil on purpose to the right side of the desk. If it wasn't coming from inside the desk, maybe there was something underneath.

He slipped out of his chair, dropped to his knees to pick up the pencil and peered at the base of the desk. Sure enough, something was wedged there, something white and soft-looking. He poked it hard with his pencil point, which made a squeak, then seemed to sink in. He'd have to wait until lunchtime or recess to fix it.

After the pencil poke, Mike's desk stayed quiet and well behaved, which was a relief, or would have been. But the kids around him kept staring and squeaking softly, barely above a whisper. It was driving Mike nuts and he wasn't sure he could wait for lunch.

When the noon bell finally rang, he dropped his heavy arithmetic book on the floor and clambered out of his seat to pick it up. As he did so, he wedged his left shoulder under the desk and shoved it sideways. Out popped a small rubber kitten, the sort of thing you might give a baby to play with. It was white, or it had been once. Now it was dirty and had a hole where Mike's pencil point had gone through the rubber.

In the bustle of kids opening and closing desks and finding their lunches, Mike gave the rubber kitten a quick squeeze. Nothing. No noise at all. So the pencil point had done the trick and silenced the beast. But not in time, of course. For the rest of the day, kids squeaked and whispered and called him Rat Boy.

Mike kept glancing at the thin, ugly face of Andy Simms and wondering how much more of this he could take. What could he do to make the guy quit bothering him?

That afternoon, as they left school, Joseph didn't mention the noises or the kids squeaking. Mike didn't know whether his friend hadn't heard, for he sat all the way across the room, or whether Joseph was just being nice. Either way, Mike wasn't about to bring it up—too embarrassing.

Instead, he concentrated on making tracks for the warehouse, where they had a real rat waiting. Maybe there'd be some good news at the end of this rotten day. But no, Old Sneaky looked healthier than ever when Mike and Joseph checked on him, so they had to make plans to hunt for a moonshiner.

21

On Herr's Island

Early Saturday morning, Mike hurried to Joseph's house. With Old Sneaky stuck in that glass jar and unable to steal the bait, Mike's traps had been full. Five pennies jingled in his pocket. As he reached 19th Street and turned toward the river, he half wished Joseph had been unlucky—that his brothers either hadn't known about any moonshiners or else hadn't been willing to tell about it. But when his pal answered the door with a wide grin on his face, Mike knew they'd be snooping.

"What did you find out?"

Buttoning his coat, Joseph stepped outside and closed the door behind him. "There's a guy nearby, over on Herr's Island on the back channel."

Mike wrinkled his nose. They slaughtered animals on Herr's Island and butchered them too. When the wind blew downriver, everybody in the Strip breathed the stench. "Eeew, Herr's Island stinks with all the cows and pigs and blood and guts."

"Sorry, but that's where the guy makes the stuff," Joseph explained. "Maybe he likes the slaughterhouse stench. It covers up any smells he makes."

Mike shook his head; he didn't want to go to the island. He stuck his hands into his coat pockets, chilled by the cold, gray day.

Joseph shoved his shoulder. "Come on, Mike, we'll have an adventure. We'll be G-men, like Eliot Ness, laying traps for the crooks." He grinned. "You're good at trapping rats, so why not crooks?"

Mike could think of about a hundred reasons, but he kept them to himself while he and Joseph made their way to 31st Street and started across the bridge.

He'd known about the stink on Herr's Island; he hadn't been prepared for the noise. As he and Joseph trotted down the sloping road that led from the bridge to the island, all he could hear were the shrill squeals of pigs, the bellows and bawls of cattle.

"Suppose they know they're going to get chopped into hamburger?" Joseph asked. "They're sure making a racket."

Mike wrinkled his nose. "If we can smell the blood, so can they. They probably know something's wrong."

"I smell more than blood," Joseph said. "There's manure here, lots of it. And whatever's coming from that smokestack." He pointed to a tall redbrick tower upstream that belched greasy-looking smoke.

"Soap factory," Mike said. "Pop says they do it all here, kill them, chop them up, turn the fat into soap and the manure and bones into fertilizer." He pointed toward the north bank of the Allegheny. "When they're all done, they haul the skins over there to the River Street Tannery and make leather. That smells terrible too."

"Aren't you glad your pop's got a food warehouse instead?" Joseph asked. "Catching rats may not be the best job in the world, but imagine working here your whole life."

Mike didn't want to think about it. No matter what Andy Simms said, the food Costa Brothers sold was clean. The meat they ground up for the sausages was already butchered and trimmed. It had never bothered Mike to imagine working in Pop's business when he got older. But a place like this? Never!

"This whole island looks like it's covered with cow pens and factories. I don't see any room for a moonshiner," Mike grumbled. He'd just as soon cross back over to the Strip and forget about Herr's Island.

"Upstream," Joseph said. "We're supposed to follow the tracks to the end of the island. The moonshiner's set up on the back channel. Come on."

The closer they got to the cow pens, the louder the bellows and the stronger the stink. Finally, they reached a roadway that ran from side to side, across the skinny part of the island. "Train track's this way," Joseph said, pointing toward the main flow of the river with the Strip beyond.

Alongside the tracks, the air felt cold but fresher. Mike balanced on one silvery rail, Joseph on the other as they headed east toward the tip of the island. Once there, they hopped down from the tracks and carefully made their way around the muddy point of land.

On the other side, a narrow channel flowed, looking more like a creek than the wide Allegheny. And just as Joseph had said, a shelf of land edged alongside the channel. On the island side of the shelf, the land rose steeply, covered with sumacs, sycamores and maples.

"Now what?" Mike asked.

"We go carefully," Joseph said, leading the way. "It's supposed to be around that first little bend."

Mike followed, stepping gently in the damp earth just inches from the lapping river. At the bend, Joseph stopped and turned back, whispering and pointing. "Jeepers, Mike. Look at that."

In a clearing to their left, Mike spied something shiny. Easing closer, he leaned into a sturdy maple and peered around the trunk. Sure enough, a guy was cooking something. He stood in the clearing, adding dead branches to a fire that blazed under a dented kettle. Above the kettle, a long copper tube poked out with curls and twists and another pot attached to the far end. Beyond the first fire and kettle, Mike could see two more. Just seeing those fires gave Mike a fit of shivers—he would have given a week's worth of ice cream money for a chance to warm his hands. He shivered again. *Brrr, ice cream, bad thing to think about right now.*

At a spot where the path widened, he took a deep breath. As Mike inhaled the cold air, he caught an unexpected scent that seemed to rise above the animal smells. "Smell that? Smoke and something sweet— almost like a bakery?"

Joseph breathed in and then nodded. "Must be the hooch. Let's creep through the trees and get closer."

Off the path, rotting branches and dead bushes grabbed at Mike's feet, but he plodded on as quietly as he could. Ahead of him, Joseph finally paused and sank to the leaf-littered dirt.

Mike crouched behind him among some thick bushes, hoping the scrub hid them well enough in the dim, gray day. But kneeling in the damp chilled him through.

As they watched, the guy moved from his first fire to his second, adding more logs. They'd found the moonshiner, all right. From what Mike could see, this guy had a big operation, for another man appeared, hauling wood for the fires.

Mike hoped the noise from the animals would cover up any small sounds they made by accident, but animals or not, he tried to sit absolutely still and even breathed carefully.

We're good at this, Mike thought after a few minutes

of watching. *And now that I've gotten used to the smell, it's okay. Maybe I should be a cop instead of working in the warehouse. Cops get paid for snooping.*

He was grinning at the thought when a loud clatter sounded behind them. Both boys jumped to their feet, and when Mike turned to see what had caused the racket, he rammed right into a skinny, mean-looking man. The guy grabbed Mike's arm with one hand and grasped Joseph's coat with the other.

"Hey, let go!"

"Not on your life, you dirty little scum. What do you think you're doing here?"

22

Caught

The man dragged them toward the fires, where the other two guys had stopped to stare. "Caught me a couple of spies, Jacko. What we gonna do with them?" He shoved hard; Mike and Joseph tumbled, sprawling to the ground.

Mike's heart was thudding. He tried to think of some way to escape, but these men were big, and plenty strong if the one who'd grabbed them was any example. Even if the river hadn't been filthy, it was a cold day to try to swim home.

The guy who seemed to be in charge stepped closer, and Mike kept staring at the muddy black boots the man wore.

134

"We're going to ask them a couple of questions. What happens after that depends on the answers. Look at me, boys. You hear?"

Mike stood and looked up. The guy called Jacko was tall and broad-shouldered. He had some sort of iron bar in his hand for tending the fire. *Or for beating up spies,* Mike thought. Still, he looked the big man in the eye.

Next to Mike, Joseph also stood and he spoke. "We heard you. Ask your questions."

"Who are you and what are you doing here?" Jacko demanded. "How did a couple of scrawny little mutts like you find out about us?"

"We're just kids; who we are don't matter," Joseph replied, his voice rough and mean-sounding.

Mike was impressed that Joseph had managed to speak at all, let alone act tough. But he realized it was their only chance, that and a good excuse. But what? They didn't dare snitch on Joseph's brothers.

"You listen in the right places," Joseph went on, "you find out what you need to know. People talk in front of kids. Sometimes they act like we've got mud in our ears and can't hear."

"So what are you doing here?"

Mike plunged in, not quite sure what he was going to say. "A kid at school . . . he . . . he dared us. Said we were too scared to find a moonshiner and get some hooch. So we came."

The guy who had caught them let out a harsh laugh. "Ha! That's the kind of thing we mighta done, years back. Huh, Jacko?"

Jacko nodded. "How was you planning to get the booze, boys? Steal it?"

Next to Mike, Joseph swaggered and straightened his shoulders. "Yeah, if we could. What's the fun of taking a dare if you don't do something real bad?"

The men laughed. "Got us a couple of live wires," the man who had caught them said. He cuffed them roughly around the shoulders.

"Don't blame you for trying, but you won't be stealing from us," Jacko said. "I could sell you some, though. Got any money?"

"A little," Mike said. He reached into his pocket and pulled out the five cents, wishing the pennies were dimes or even quarters.

"I got some too," Joseph said. He fished out a nickel.

"Ten cents. Boy, what a pair of big spenders," the man who had caught them said. "What shall we do, just lighten their pockets and send them home to Mama?"

"Nah, we'll sell them a little. Who knows, they might grow up and turn into real customers." Jacko reached into his pocket and took out a small glass bottle, a little more than half full. He held out his other hand, palm up, for the money. "Here you go, boys, pay up and the hooch is yours."

Mike tossed his pennies into the man's hand. Joseph did the same with his nickel, and Jacko's thick fingers curled into a fist around the money. Mike reached for the bottle, but the man held it back.

136

"Just one more little detail, and the bottle is yours. Who's the kid? The one who conned you into this trick?"

Mike opened his mouth to speak, but his throat went dry and only air came out. Beside him, Joseph stood like a block of wood.

"Well, you want this bottle or not? Who's the kid? I gotta plug up the leaks in my security. I'm not running a Sunday school; I can't have a bunch of kids showing up every day. Gimme a name."

They couldn't rat on Joseph's brothers; they just couldn't. Mike found his voice. "Nobody important, sir. Just a . . . a dumb kid."

"I need a name." Jacko's face went hard.

Oh, geez, what now? Mike thought. He knew they'd be in worse trouble if they didn't say something fast. He blurted out the first thing that came to mind. "Okay. I'll tell you. He's the dumbest kid we know. His name is Simms. Andy Simms."

As the words left his mouth, Mike smiled. He hadn't planned it or anything, but maybe he'd just given that Simms a dose of his own medicine and Simms would be the one squeaking now.

"You want to taste it?" Joseph held out the bottle of moonshine to Mike as the boys hurried across the bridge and back to their side of the river.

"Nah," Mike said. "Remember, it could have poison in it. That's why we got it."

Joseph stuck the bottle back into his coat pocket. "Right. After that whopper we spun for those moonshiners, I forgot about Old Sneaky. Suppose he'll like it?"

"We'll find out soon," Mike said. They scurried along until they reached 22nd Street. Crossing to the alley, Mike led the way to the back entrance of the warehouse and slid open the door. "Shhh, quiet now so Pop won't hear us," he said.

When they reached the cellar and Mike picked up the pickle jar, the rat reared back like it wanted to attack through the glass.

"He's sure in a bad mood," Joseph said. "Good thing the glass jar is thick."

"You bet," Mike agreed. "Look, I'll hold the jar, you pour in the hooch." Old Sneaky clawed at the glass, making Mike shiver.

Joseph uncorked the bottle and drizzled the pale liquid through a hole in the lid, into the empty can in the bottom of the pickle jar.

Still the rat bared its teeth, but by the time Joseph had finished pouring, the smell must have gotten through, for the critter started slurping up the hooch.

"Wow, look at that," Joseph said. "He's drinking that stuff faster than you can drink a milk shake at Klavon's."

Mike watched until the rat stopped drinking. Old Sneaky sure seemed to like hooch, and once he'd filled his belly, he curled up for a nap.

"You think he's going to die, or just sleep?" Joseph asked.

Mike remembered what Pop had said a few days ago about his cheese. "I don't know, Joseph. But if he does die, I have a feeling he'll die happy. I think we've got ourselves one drunk rat."

23

Drunk as a Skunk

On Sundays nobody went to work at Costa Brothers, so after church Mike had to spend the rest of the day catching up on his homework and wondering about Old Sneaky. Partway through the afternoon, Tony called up the attic stairs to him. "Hey, Mike. Got a minute?"

Mike popped out of his room, glad to forget about long division for a while. "Sure, what's up?"

"Come here, I got something for you."

Mike took the steps two at a time and followed Tony into his room on the second floor. When he got there, he blinked hard. Tony's room was usually piled high with clothes and newspapers, magazines and odd things he'd picked up in the Strip. Today, except for the bed, the room looked completely clean. And even the bed was neat, for Tony. Folded-up clothing lay on top in three tidy piles.

"What's going on?"

"Packing. I leave for West Virginia next Saturday. The CCC, remember?"

Mutely, Mike nodded. He'd been doing his best to forget about the CCC. With Old Sneaky to fuss over, he'd mostly succeeded. "Next Saturday? So soon?" He could hear his voice crack and he hated it.

"Yep. They're taking a whole busload of us down." Tony punched him lightly on the shoulder. "Come on, kid. It's West Virginia, not the North Pole. I get leave time. Besides, I've got something for you."

He reached into his closet and pulled out his brown leather jacket with the sheepskin lining, the one that looked like it belonged to an airplane pilot.

"You've gotta be kidding!" Mike said. "That's your best . . . your favorite . . . I can't just take it."

"Consider it a loan," Tony said with a smile.

He tossed the jacket and Mike made a quick catch.

"They give us uniforms, everything from Skivvies to coats and boots. So I was hoping you'd sorta look after this for me until I get back. Wear it and keep the leather oiled and smooth. Go ahead, try it on for size."

Swallowing hard, Mike slipped his arms inside the jacket. The lining felt warm and soft against his chest, the outside cold and smooth to his fingertips. The sleeves were only a little too long.

"Here, there's a strap to tighten the cuffs," Tony said, pulling the leather closer around Mike's wrists. "Not bad, Mike. Not quite as handsome as me, but pretty swell for a kid."

"I . . . Wow, Tony." Mike jammed his hands into the roomy pockets. "I'll take real good care of it for you. I promise."

"I know you will, Mike. And there's another thing I'd like you to promise me, before I leave. It's the old man. I heard about the night you found him outside wandering around. Keep an eye open for me, will you? Write and let me know how he's doing? Don't sugar-coat it, either. I want the truth, unvarnished."

"Sure. Of course I'll write." The thought made Mike's eyes sting and he knew he'd start bawling like a baby if he didn't get away from the too-neat room and the folded-up clothes. "Thanks for the jacket, Tony. I gotta go back and finish that darned arithmetic or Sister will have my hide." He ran for the stairs, but even though he had on Tony's best jacket, he felt cold, the inside kind of cold that might never warm up.

Monday morning came at last and Mike couldn't wait to check on Old Sneaky instead of imagining how empty the house would be in a week. When he made his way into the warehouse cellar and dug out the pickle jar, at first he thought they'd found the answer.

The rat didn't move; it just lay in the bottom like a lump of cold lard.

When Mike carried the glass jar closer to the light, however, he could see the faint rise and fall of the animal's side that meant Old Sneaky was just sleeping. Sleeping soundly and hung over most likely, Mike decided. The glass jar looked pretty nasty in the good light, so he set it down and went hunting for a cleaner one.

The rat was sleeping so hard, Mike was able to pull out the tin can they'd used for water without waking him. Once he'd rinsed and refilled that, he lifted the lid again and grabbed the rat's tail. That startled Old Sneaky—he squeaked as Mike lifted him out of the dirty jar and into the clean one. Once settled into the fresh jar, though, he curled right back up to sleep.

"Drunk as a skunk," Mike muttered to himself. He tossed in a hunk of cheese rind and screwed the old holey lid tightly onto the new jar. When he picked it up, the old jar gave off such a stench that he set it beside the door to the loading dock so he could dump it outside in a trash bin. Then he made his rounds and found only two full traps, but at least he'd found two.

A few minutes later, with the old jar thrown away, he hurried up Penn Avenue to meet Joseph. The sun was trying to break through a patchy layer of clouds and Mike couldn't help smiling. A sunny day in November and money in his pocket—two good omens at one time.

"Well?" Joseph asked. "What's the news?"

"Still breathing," Mike said.

"Did he look sick?"

"Nope, hung over maybe. I even felt sorry for him and changed the jar so he wouldn't have to sleep in his mess."

"Good thinking. But if Old Sneaky's still breathing, that moonshiner isn't poisoning anybody."

"Maybe not," Mike agreed. "Or maybe the rat's just going to take a while to die. Either way, we can't do anything about it right now. We've got to get to school, and fast."

The third good omen came as they stood by their desks while Sister called the class to order a few minutes later. The spot next to Mike stood empty—Andy Simms was absent. *So maybe we're on the right track,* Mike told himself as he opened his speller. *Maybe this afternoon Old Sneaky will die and we'll have our answer. Yes, sir, three good omens pointing to the final treasure.* And with that, he began to copy the week's spelling words five times apiece in careful rows.

In spite of good omens, Sneaky was alive and healthy when Mike checked him on Monday afternoon and again on Tuesday morning.

"It's not the moonshine," Mike told Joseph as they walked up Penn Avenue toward school early Tuesday.

"And it wasn't river water, either," Joseph said, shaking his head. "That uses up the drinks idea. So

we've got to figure out what your grandpap, those hobos who died and a whole bunch of rats could have
eaten. You sure we can't just ask your grandpap?"

Mike thought it over. "We could try. He might tell
us what he had for breakfast today, or he might tell
us about a picnic he had when he was twelve. You
never know."

"That must be tough," Joseph said.

Mike shrugged. On the good days he could convince himself that Grandpap was fine, but the bad days
were getting harder to ignore.

"Maybe we can spy on the old man," Joseph sug-
gested. "Watch what he eats and then if he gets sick
we'll know what caused it."

Mike shook his head. "That would be fine if this
were summer and we didn't have school every day. But
we can't watch him when we're in school."

"Your mother's around and your aunt lives next
door, doesn't she, Mike? Your uncle Frank's wife?"

"Yeah, but they're busy. Mom has lots to do taking
care of all of us guys, and my aunt, well, she's not feeling too great herself. Aunt Marie's gonna hatch me a
cousin one of these days, so she has to rest a lot. And
Grandpap can be sneaky. When he's in the right mood,
he just slips away. Sometimes he goes into the warehouse with Pop, but other times, who knows where
he goes?"

Mike let out a big sigh. All this talk about Grandpap was hard; he hated explaining about the bad times.

He hadn't realized how much he'd been counting on either the river water or the moonshine causing the trouble.

Joseph kicked at a rough scrap of wood that lay on the sidewalk. "Okay, so we can't watch him, Mike. What can we do? Isn't there something?"

Mike thought hard. "Only thing I can tell you is that he hasn't gotten sick since the day of the banana explosion—that was a Friday, in the evening. At least not that I know about. So whatever it was that made him sick, he hasn't had any for over a week."

"It's got to be some kind of food," Joseph said. "All we have to do is figure out what. And we do know stuff. We know it isn't something your mother cooks or else the rest of your family would get sick. And it's not that soup Father Cox gives the hobos, since only two guys died. So it has to be something else, food they picked up on the street. That helps, doesn't it?"

Mike frowned. "It would help if we lived in a fancy neighborhood like the Mellon Patch up in Highland Park. But look around you, Joseph. There's food everywhere, and more coming in every night on the trains. Sure we can test some with Old Sneaky, but where do we start? It's hopeless."

21

Andy Simms

Mike's temper only worsened as they crossed the schoolyard. Andy Simms was back, looking meaner than ever and sporting a bruise on his left cheek. He headed straight for Mike and stopped him near the school steps.

"Hey, you, Rat Boy." Simms grabbed Mike's arm and pinched it hard. "You lose your marbles or something? What's the idea of telling some moonshiner my name?"

Mike yanked his arm away, stepped closer and grinned. He'd gotten Simms in big trouble. It had just happened, almost by itself. Nice. "What did he do, come looking for you? Pop you one in the face?"

"My face is my business, Rat Boy."

"Hey, Simms, how did the moonshiner find you?" Joseph asked.

"He knows my ma and told her a couple of dumb guys came trying to buy some booze."

"What makes you think it was us?" Mike demanded.

"The guy said it was some redheaded Irish kid and a greasy wop. Sound familiar?"

"Nobody calls me that. Watch your mouth, Simms, or *I'll* pop you. One good bruise deserves another." Mike shoved him hard on the shoulder.

"Save it for after school, Costa, when no Sisters can come and rescue you," Simms muttered.

Mike spat in the dirt. "Fine with me."

Simms turned to Joseph. "If you know what's good for you, Ryan, you'll make yourself scarce this afternoon. Either way, it don't matter. I'll have *all* my pals with me this time and we'll fight one of you or ten of you." He shook his fist in Joseph's face, then shoved past and charged into school.

Later, while he was supposed to be working on his arithmetic problems, Mike scribbled a note to Joseph. *Let's get reinforcements at recess so we can paste them after school.* He snapped his pencil point on purpose; then on the way to the sharpener he dropped the note onto Joseph's desk.

At lunch, the two of them talked it over. "I got a better idea," Joseph said. "You stay here and I go on home, like Simms said. But then I come back with my brothers and your uncles."

"Nah, they're too old; we can't let them fight for us. I'm ready."

"I'm not, not if there are ten of them," Joseph said. "Let's duck and we'll think of something. At least let's talk to my brothers; they'll show us some good moves."

"Maybe." Mike had his doubts. Since Simms had probably gotten that bruise on his cheek from the moonshiner, he'd be out for revenge. Why not just take care of it, get it over with? He stretched out his fingers and slowly curled them into a fist.

But no matter what Mike said, he couldn't convince Joseph to fight a big battle until they'd gotten pointers from his brothers, so that afternoon Mike had to duck. When Sister Mary John finally opened the classroom door and dismissed them, Joseph went home right away. Mike lingered at his desk, taking time to pack up his schoolbooks, tidy loose papers and plan his escape.

As the classroom cleared, Mike figured Simms would be collecting his buddies. By the time Mike marched out the front door, there'd be a bunch of tough guys waiting in the first alley to ambush him. The very thought made his temper boil up again.

Maybe I'll just go ahead and fight all of them on my own, he told himself. *Who needs Joseph, anyway? Simms is my enemy.*

He slammed book after book into his desk and imagined the faces grinning at him from that alley, nine or ten of them. He sighed. *Nah, can't fight today, it'll be a massacre. I'll have to wait for Joseph, but boy, by tomorrow, my fists are gonna fly. . . .*

But that was the next day; today Mike needed a hideout. The older boys' lavatory stood directly across the hall from Sister Mary John's classroom and he slipped inside as quietly as he could. He'd lock himself in a stall for an hour if he had to, until Simms and his gang got tired of waiting.

But as he rounded the corner and sped toward the row of stalls, he stopped short. Andy Simms was there, bent over one of the sinks.

Mike froze and tensed his muscles, getting ready. Luck was with him for once—he'd caught Simms alone and the gang was probably waiting outside.

Fine, let them wait. He and Simms could finish it here and now, just the two of them, Sisters or no Sisters. He stepped closer, ready to toss a punch, then heard a gagging noise as Simms bent over farther.

Simms is sick? Even as Mike took a step backward, Simms heaved and lost his lunch into the sink. Some of the mess splashed out onto the floor. The smell made Mike's stomach jump and he covered his nose and mouth with one hand.

Mike didn't want to look, but he couldn't seem to help himself. Simms kept on puking and the smell got worse and worse. This was probably why he'd missed school the day before, Mike realized. *And I'll miss school tomorrow if I don't get out of here fast. Phew!*

His stomach rumbled and twisted, and he took another step backward toward the door. Simms heaved again, and Mike's breath caught as another batch splashed onto the floor. He stared. This time the vomit was mixed with blood. Like Grandpap's. The old man's face, wrinkled in pain, flashed before his eyes.

Without a sound, Mike eased himself out of the bathroom, his mind racing. *Could it be true? Is Andy Simms sick just like Grandpap was? I've got to talk to Joseph right away.*

But before he could talk to Joseph, Mike needed to get away from school and Simms' buddies. If the gang was still waiting for him, they'd be expecting him to head down Penn Avenue.

So he'd fool them; he'd head up the avenue toward town and cut over to Smallman Street. He ran down the hall and slipped out the door, ducking along the edge of the school building until he reached 13th Street.

There he crossed over Penn and made tracks for Smallman and home. As he raced up the pavement, he could feel himself grinning. He'd done it, all right, he'd escaped Simms and the ambush.

At 19th Street Mike stopped outside Joseph's house to catch his breath. He raised his fist to knock, then stopped for a moment. *Wait a minute,* he realized with a start, *Simms' being sick is good. If we can get him to talk, his brain, puny as it is, won't forget what he ate like Grandpap's does. So we can find out what's making people sick. But first we've got to get him to talk.*

Again, Mike thanked whatever lucky stars had picked him to shine on. Not every kid had somebody like Joseph for a friend. At a time like this, when they had to squeeze information out of Simms' puny hide, Mike blessed Joseph for having a cop for a father. If that day in the shantytown was any example, Joseph could ask questions like a real detective.

25

Interrogation

By the next morning, Mike and Joseph had a plan. They hurried past St. Patrick's School and waited on the corner of 13th Street so they could corner Simms before he arrived. If they were lucky, they'd catch him alone, without any of his friends to get in the way.

Sure enough, after they'd waited ten minutes, he came trudging up Penn Avenue. Mike stood on one side, Joseph on the other, and each grabbed Simms by an arm and steered him down 13th Street and into a littered alleyway behind a building that sold metal pipe.

"Hey, let go of me!" Simms tried to elbow Mike in the ribs.

"We just want to ask you a couple of questions," Joseph said. "Give us the right answers and we'll never bother you again."

"Says you!" Simms shot back. "Come on, let me go." He twisted his arms, trying to free them.

Mike held on. "Yesterday afternoon you got sick. In the bathroom."

"Did not."

"Did too, I saw you. What did you eat for lunch?"

"None of your business, Macaroni Boy. None of your wop food, that's for sure."

"Come on, it's important. What'd you eat for lunch?" Joseph stepped closer and stuck his face right into Simms'.

Simms tried to butt Joseph with his head, but Mike held on tight.

"You guys ain't too smart, you know. I already owed you a beating after you spilled my name to that moonshiner. You got me in plenty of hot water. Now I'm gonna have to whip you twice." He thrashed again and almost slipped free, but Mike clamped his thin arm with the fingers of both hands.

He studied Simms' face. It looked skinnier than ever, and the bruise on his cheek looked bluer than it had the day before. That moonshiner had been tough enough to leave marks. Mike was about ready to haul back and leave marks of his own when a door opened and a man came outside, waving a broom at them.

"Scram, you punks, or I'll smack you."

With that, Simms twisted again, wrenched free and tore off toward school.

"So much for talking to Andy Simms," Joseph said. "We couldn't even hold on to him. I still say we need to get my brothers and your uncles to help. They can beat it out of him."

"Nah," Mike said. He pounded his right fist against the palm of his left hand. "It won't work."

"But they can," Joseph insisted. "They haul crates of food every night; they're plenty strong."

"Come on, we'll talk later. We'd better get moving or we'll be late."

All that day, as he tried to pay attention to Sister Mary John, Mike tested out different ideas in his mind. He and Joseph had sure messed up their chance to make Simms talk, so more of that wouldn't work.

Joseph's brothers and Mike's uncles were strong—they could beat up anybody—but Mike figured a beating would backfire and make Simms zip his lip. He could try to get Pop to talk to Simms' folks, but Pop's temper could heat up too, and the grown-ups might get into a fight.

"Mark my words, Michael Costa. A day will come when you're in a tough spot . . . and fighting won't help. It will only make things worse." Mom's words came to Mike as clear as the school bell, stopping him cold. *No fighting. I've got to try something else. But what?*

His mind went blank for a moment; then a crazy

idea came to him. "Oh no," Mike muttered to himself. *Not that. I couldn't . . .*

But the more he fought against it, the more sense it made, even if he hated the idea. It felt like Mom was inside his head, preaching at him again, but he couldn't stop the thoughts from coming.

If you wanted somebody's help, you had to act polite, even if he was the scum of the earth. You had to tell him your reasons, and have something to trade for information. And you had to talk to him yourself, one on one, not outnumber him or gang up, which meant Mike would have to do this part alone, without any help from Joseph.

Mike peered sideways as Simms hunched over the map he was drawing. He wore raggedy knickers that looked too small and his socks had holes. Sure, other kids in Mike's class were poor, but as Mike glanced around the classroom he realized that Simms looked the worst. Trouble was, Mike didn't have any cash to pay for information.

Maybe he could just tell Simms about Grandpap. And it would be a trade, for if Simms knew what was making Grandpap sick, he'd know to stop eating or drinking the stuff himself.

Mike frowned. A thin plan, but it was the best he could come up with. When school let out, he made his excuses to Joseph, then hurried up Penn Avenue toward downtown. By the time he'd crossed 12th Street, he caught sight of Simms half a block ahead.

Mike slowed down and decided to keep that half

block between them. He hoped Simms wouldn't stop and turn around before he got home. Mike was counting on catching Simms with his folks around so the two of them wouldn't end up in another fight.

At 11th Street, Simms turned right. Mike sped up and followed, just in time to see Simms slip into a narrow alley between two brick buildings. Mike hurried to the alley and watched him climb a rickety set of steps a few yards away.

Where's he going? Mike wondered. This wasn't a house; it was the back side of a store that sold cleaning products. Still, Simms climbed the stairs, opened a door and disappeared inside.

Mike stood on the sidewalk, weighing his choices. If Simms had a job, he would still be safe enough, for a boss would be around. Stepping carefully over a mess of rusting tin cans, Mike made his way up the alley and grabbed the railing of the steps.

It wasn't a real staircase, just a fire escape, but he climbed it anyway. At the top, he pounded on the door before he could lose his nerve. The door opened and Mike found himself looking into the face of a skinny, pale woman who was clutching a dark sweater around herself.

"What do you want?"

"I'm looking for Andy Simms. He's in my class and he . . . he forgot a book in school today." Mike hefted his schoolbooks like he'd brought one for Simms. "Sister will get real mad if he doesn't finish the map."

Mike itched with all the lies he was telling, but

the woman didn't seem to notice. "Come in, then," she said.

Mike stepped into a dark, shadowy room with two beds along one wall. A couple of rickety chairs stood on bare floorboards on the other side of the room, and that was about all Mike could see.

"Andy. Somebody to see you."

From somewhere in a back corner a door opened and Simms stepped out. "You? What are you doing here?"

Mike's mouth felt dry. "I . . . um, I brought you something from school."

Simms glanced at the woman, then scowled at Mike. "Come on, out on the steps." He shoved past and opened the door.

Mike had no choice but to follow Simms outside, where he stood at the top of the stairs, blocking Mike's way down.

Simms grabbed Mike's arm and pinched it hard. "What's the idea, following me home? Nobody follows me home."

"Sorry. It's important." Mike wanted to wrench free, but the fire escape felt even more rickety with two kids standing on it.

Simms shoved him back against the brick wall. "Yeah, sure. It's important. You just want to snoop out where I live so you can tell the guys at school. Try it and you'll be sorry." He stretched the fingers of his right hand and slowly curled them into a fist.

Mike held his hand in front of his face. "No. I don't . . . I won't tell anybody. That's not why I came." His breath was coming in fast bursts, like he'd just run a mile. If he didn't get this right, Simms would start pounding on him, and it was a long way to the ground.

"It's my grandpap," he explained, clutching the railing of the fire escape. "He's been throwing up blood. Just like you did yesterday. And those hobos who died . . . the cops saw bloody vomit and thought the men had been throwing up too. . . ." Mike's voice gave out. Simms folded his arms across his chest and stared.

"Come on, Simms. Andy, I need your help, bad."

"You need my help? That's a good one. I ain't helping you, Rat Boy, Macaroni Boy, Dumb Boy. You and me, we're enemies and nothing's going to change that."

Macaroni Boy, that again! Mike closed his eyes. Part of him wanted to punch this kid, toss him over the railing of the fire escape and break his head. They were enemies. Nothing would ever change that.

He opened his eyes and stared at Simms, who had an ugly sneer on his face. Mike glared, unwilling to look away. *Macaroni Boy, all that talk about rats in sausages. Why's he always picking on me? What did I ever do to him?* Mike wondered.

And then, as if he'd turned the dial and tuned into a radio station, the static in his mind cleared and he heard the answer. *I picked the first fight—that day in the schoolyard when I bloodied his nose. Then I threw a rat at him on the playground; that's lots worse than rotten apples. And I'm still at it, giving his name to that moonshiner. I started it, I helped keep it going, now I've got to end it, but how? With a guy like Simms, talk doesn't work any better than fighting.*

Mike and Simms continued to study each other, like it was a contest and whoever broke off the staring first would lose. Mike noticed dark shadows under Simms' eyes. His face looked awfully skinny, with bony cheeks poking out and a pointy chin.

Maybe there was more to it than who started the feud, Mike thought. Simms looked so thin, like he didn't eat often enough, and he lived in that small bare room above a store. *And me, I have a big family and a nice house, and most of all, I have food. Plenty to eat.*

No sooner had the thoughts formed than Mike knew what to do. He could get Andy Simms to talk and neither of them would end up with a bloody nose for once. *He's right. I am Macaroni Boy. Thank goodness.*

26

Fair Trade

"Look, Simms, I've got a deal for you. You tell me what I want to know, I'll pay you."

"Cold cash? How much?" Simms was still frowning, but his eyes had opened slightly and Mike was sure he had the boy's attention.

"Not cash. I don't have any. I'll trade you food for answers."

"You crazy? I don't want any of that nasty I-talian stuff. None of your rat sausages either."

Mike's temper boiled up inside, but he swallowed it. "How about plain old macaroni and cheese? Look, I'll bring you two pounds of cheese and five of macaroni."

"Twice that," Simms countered.

Mike scowled. Either way he was going to have to snitch food from Pop's shelves; it didn't really matter how much.

"Okay, twice that. But I need to know what made you sick yesterday. I need to know everything. What did you have for breakfast and lunch? Supper the night before? Don't leave anything out."

Simms looked away and scuffed his foot against the fire escape floor. "Let's see, I had caviar and champagne for breakfast."

"Come on, no fooling around."

"All right, I'll tell, but you gotta promise to keep it to yourself."

Mike shrugged. "Sure. Okay."

"For breakfast, I had—" Simms stopped and snorted. "Rich boy like you, you're just gonna laugh."

Being hungry was nothing to laugh about, Mike thought. But saying that aloud would only get Simms more riled up. "Come on, quit stalling."

Simms looked away. "Breakfast and lunch I had lard sandwiches."

Mike clamped down his jaw, but tried not to let his face show how greasy and nasty that sounded. "How about supper the night before?"

"Catfish."

"From the market? Which one?"

"Oh, sure, rich boy. My ma and me, we've got tons of money, we go to all the markets. Only the finest . . ."

Mike ignored the wise remarks. "Where'd you get the fish?"

"Where do you think? I caught them. In the river. There's a depression on, you know. Folks gotta eat, and catfish and carp, they're free."

Mike closed his eyes and remembered sitting on the back step, watching Grandpap gut those fish he'd caught. *Bingo! Grandpap's always catching fish out there on the river and making Mom cook it up for him. Nobody else in the family likes the stuff and nobody else is getting sick. The hobos could have eaten it and so could the rats—they'll eat anything, even old fish heads with rotten bananas for dessert.*

But before Mike could even finish these thoughts, doubts filled his mind. They'd tested the river water and it hadn't hurt Old Sneaky, so how could the fish have been poisoned? Bad as the water was, that idea didn't make sense unless . . . unless you had to drink a whole lot of it for the poison to work. Shoot, the fish didn't just take a drink now and then, they lived in it every minute of the day. Maybe that made a difference. Or maybe there was something bad hidden deep at the bottom of the river.

"You got any catfish left?" Mike asked.

"There was some, but I had it for lunch yesterday, with the sandwich."

Lunch the day before. And then Simms had gotten sick after school; that seemed about right to Mike. "What about your mom? Has she been sick?"

"Some. Not as much as me, but she usually gives

me more of the fish. Since I'm a kid, you know."
Simms picked at a hangnail on his thumb.

Mike did know. He'd seen his mom divide up the
meatballs, saving only a small one for herself.

Finally Simms looked Mike in the eye again.
"Costa? You really think there's something wrong with
the fish?"

"Only one way to find out. I'll go get your macaroni and cheese if you'll catch another catfish." Mike
stuck out his hand. "Deal?"

Simms ignored the hand but nodded. "Deal. Give
me an hour."

An hour was plenty of time for Mike to make a
round-trip to 22nd Street and help himself to macaroni and cheese. With any luck, Pop would be busy
and wouldn't notice what Mike was up to. Still,
when he arrived at the warehouse, he sneaked in the
back door.

Standing on the bottom step, he listened and heard
footsteps above his head at the front of the building.
Slowly, stepping as lightly as he could to keep from
making noise, Mike crept up the stairs. At the top he
shoved open the cellar door and peered out.

He was in luck. Pop had a pail and some rags and
was washing the brand-new front window. The icebox
stood close to the basement steps, and if Pop turned
around, Mike could pretend he was helping himself to
dry cheese rinds for his traps.

Carefully, he pulled on the icebox handle and

opened the door. He grabbed the first good-sized round of cheese he found. He wasn't sure about the weight, but Simms probably didn't have a scale anyhow. Easing the icebox door shut, he tiptoed back down the stairs and set the cheese inside a clean wooden crate.

Now for the macaroni. Mike counted to ten to calm his nerves, then retraced his steps. At the top of the cellar stairs, he paused again and peered out. His luck was holding—Pop had more than half the window still to wash.

Mike crept along the wooden floor to the back of the building, where the big sacks of macaroni lined the shelves. Again, he didn't stop to worry about what kind of noodles to snitch; he just grabbed a bag, hugged it to his chest and made his way back to the cellar door.

Once he reached the stairs, Mike stopped to catch his breath. He sure wasn't cut out for the life of a thief, he realized. It would probably take a week for his heart to stop thumping so hard.

He'd climbed halfway down when the door at the top creaked open. Mike turned to see Pop standing there with his hands on his hips, a dark shadow in a white apron.

"Well, Michael. Glad to see you're so hard at work. Tell me, son, do the rats like macaroni and cheese in those traps?"

"I . . . um . . ." Mike's throat froze. He could feel his legs wobble, and unless he hung on to the railing, he'd probably fall down the steps. That might be better than facing Pop.

Pop started down toward him, and Mike somehow managed to get to the bottom where his crate sat, with the round of cheese in plain sight. He set down the sack of macaroni.

"What's going on? Why are you stealing food? Doesn't your mother feed you enough?" Pop switched on the electric lights, then hauled two large barrels under one of the lights. He nudged Mike toward one. "Sit. Talk."

Mike eased himself onto the top of the barrel and tried to figure out what to say. "There's a kid at school. He's been sick like Grandpap. Vomiting blood. I finally got him to tell me what he's been eating, but I promised him macaroni and cheese in trade."

"What? Are you turning into some kind of doctor? Figuring out what makes people sick? That's crazy, Mike. And doctors get paid for their services; they don't pay the sick person."

"But it's for Grandpap," Mike said, knowing how shaky his voice sounded. He started at the beginning then and explained everything—the fights, the dead rats, the hobos, even the moonshiners.

"I think you and Joseph need to have your heads examined," Pop said. "And where's this sneaky rat you've been testing your ideas on? Here, in my warehouse?"

Mike nodded miserably.

"This I gotta see. Go. Get him."

Mike's throat and mouth felt so dry he could barely swallow. When he brought the pickle jar and set it in front of Pop, Old Sneaky sat up and peered through the glass.

"This is really something. We got a depression going on, and my son makes a pet of a rat. Feeds him good food while I'm watching every penny."

"I . . . I'm sorry, Pop. Maybe it's a bad idea, but I had to do something. And I was going to pay you back for the food I took, honest."

Pop looked Mike in the eye, then turned to examine the macaroni and cheese. "That's a lot of rat catching, boy. You'll be lucky if you ever get another nickel for ice cream."

"Yes, sir. But I've gotta do it. I've gotta go give Simms the food, or else. Please, Pop. And once I get that fish, I'll feed it to Old Sneaky."

"In my clean food warehouse?"

"Wherever you want, Pop. Only we have to give it a try. The hobos died. We've been finding dead rats everywhere. Grandpap, he got so sick."

"Most of what's the matter with your grandpap is up here," Pop said sadly, tapping his forehead. "And a fish isn't going to matter much, one way or another. Even if we find out there's something wrong with the fish, it's not going to give the old man his mind back."

"But it might make his stomach stop hurting. Please, Pop. Just let me try. If I'm wrong, I'll make it up to you. I'll take on Tony's work on Saturdays. Next summer too. I'll do anything."

"I still think you need to have your head examined," Pop said. "But go on. There's a chance, I suppose. . . ." He shook his finger in Mike's face. "No monkey business. I'm keeping an eye on this rat. You bring that fish back here and toss it in the jar; then I'm putting it someplace safe for the night. Hear me?"

"Yes, Pop. Sure, Pop. Thanks, Pop."

Before Pop could change his mind, Mike snatched up the macaroni and cheese and escaped. He ran up Penn Avenue toward 11th Street like Joseph's pop and a whole squad of cops were on his tail.

At Simms' place, he quickly hauled the food up the rickety fire escape and pounded on the door. Simms answered and spoke in whispers. "Told my ma I'd picked up a one-time job, sweeping, so she wouldn't think I was stealing. Not a word, Costa."

"Fine with me. Where's the fish?"

Simms handed him a torn paper sack. "Remember, not a word."

Mike nodded, took a quick look at the fish, clutched the sack and hurried back to the warehouse. This time, he entered by the front door and Pop sat behind the cash register, waiting for him.

From behind the counter, Pop pulled out the pickle jar and Old Sneaky. "You really think this is going to show something?"

Mike shrugged. "I don't know. We have to try it."

Pop unscrewed the lid and Mike slipped the fish

into the jar. Old Sneaky backed away at first, but quickly sank his teeth into the side of the catfish. Mike looked away.

Pop stowed the jar under the counter, then slid a slip of paper toward Mike. "I made up a bill," he said. "You sign it like an IOU. Then every time you do some work, we mark it on the back until you're paid up."

Mike took the pencil from the counter and signed the paper. When he saw the amount, more than three bucks, he realized he'd be hungry for ice cream for weeks—months maybe. And all for the sake of his enemy, Andy Simms. It just didn't seem right.

From the back of the warehouse, Mike heard the rattle of a truck engine. Uncle Frank, the last person in the world Mike wanted to see, had just arrived.

Pop cocked his head like he was listening. "We'll check the rat first thing in the morning," he said. "Until then, we'll leave the rest of the family out of this. You got any questions?"

Pop's acting fair, Mike thought. *Fairer than I deserve. And if Old Sneaky does get sick, maybe the family won't have to know I stole from the business.* But one thing still bothered him.

"Yeah, Pop, one question. How did you catch me? I didn't make any noise at all."

"You didn't have to make noise, boy. I saw you, plain as day."

"But your back was turned. You were washing the window."

"Eyes in the back of my head, son."

"Come on, Pop. How'd you see me?"

"Like you said, I was washing the window."

"So?"

"Michael, my boy. I was staring right into the glass. Haven't you ever heard of reflections?"

27

Catfish

The evening went on forever. Mom tuned the radio to her favorite program and opera music poured out, pounding away in Mike's head. Pop kept his promise and didn't mention Old Sneaky or the stolen food, but more than once, Mike caught Pop staring at him and felt his cheeks redden.

What if I've just made a fool of myself? he worried. *What if I've given away a lot of food for nothing and the uncles find out? They'll never let me forget it. I'll be fifty years old and they'll still be teasing me.*

Mike welcomed bedtime, when he could escape upstairs, but sleep brought rough dreams. Hundreds of hobos piled off freight trains . . . set up bonfires by the river . . . roasted bunches of green bananas over the flames . . . threw them into the water. . . . Huge catfish caught the bananas and carried them off. . . . Moonshiners with stills ten feet tall took ice cream and catfish and bananas and rats and cooked them into muddy whiskey. . . . And in every dream, a shadow hovered, off to one side, drinking and eating, a shadow that reminded Mike of Grandpap.

Finally, in the gray hour before sunrise, Mike got up and dressed. No sleep was better than those dreams, he decided. And he'd be ready whenever Pop wanted to go to the warehouse.

When he'd made his way to the kitchen, he was surprised to find his father there cradling a cup of coffee in his big hands. "Bad night?" Pop asked.

Mike nodded.

"I didn't sleep too well myself, son. Shall we get it over with?"

"Yes. Please."

He and Pop bundled against the early morning chill and headed up Penn Avenue. As they neared the warehouse, the bustle of men and carts filled the streets. Any other morning, Mike would have loved it, loved being a part of the buying and selling that made his neighborhood one of a kind. But today all he could think about was Old Sneaky.

When they reached the front door, Pop didn't bother with his usual opening-up comments; he just pulled out his key and unlocked it.

Mike flipped on the electric lights and darted for the counter, but Pop beat him to it.

"Here goes nothing," Pop said, bending to retrieve the pickle jar.

Mike stepped closer, wondering what they'd see.

"Looks like he ate plenty," Pop said, pointing toward the chewed remains of the catfish. "For all the good it did him."

Mike examined the jar. Old Sneaky lay on one side, his legs splayed out and his head twisted back. The rat's belly had swelled up, whether from eating too much or from poison, Mike wasn't sure. "He looks bad, Pop."

"Looks dead to me." Pop tapped the side of the jar and one of Old Sneaky's front legs twitched.

"Not dead, but close to it. Pop, it means the fish made him sick." Mike tried to grin, but the sight of Old Sneaky lying there in pain made that impossible. "Can I put him out of his misery?"

"Not yet," Pop said. "Let me think." He set the jar back under the counter and strode over to the window he'd so carefully cleaned the day before. Hands on his hips, he stared out into the street for a few minutes, then turned back to Mike. "We're going to have a busy morning, son. You, me, all the Costas."

Pop hit the release button on the cash register. "First things first," he said as the money drawer popped open. From the back of the cash tray, he pulled out a slip of paper, the one Mike had signed yesterday afternoon.

"My IOU?"

"That's right." Pop tore the paper in half and then

in half again, letting the pieces drift down into the wastebasket behind the counter. "I'm the one who owes you, Mike. We all do. Yesterday I thought you were some kind of fool. Today, I know better. You're a good son, Michael Costa."

Pop tapped Mike's forehead. "You got a smart head on your shoulders. But more." He thumped Mike on the chest. "You use your head and your heart. The rest of us, all we could hear was the old man's complaining. You went beyond." Pop's eyes glistened.

Mike stood straighter, letting the words wash away the long night's worry. "Now what?" he finally asked.

"Like I said, we got a busy morning. Soon as Franco shows up, we talk to my brothers. Then you and I take the truck and haul the rat and the fish up to the doctors at the hospital. If there's something in catfish that's been poisoning folks, the doctors will find it. After that we stop by the station house and find Daniel Ryan to tell him what we suspect."

"Can we stop and talk to Father Cox? So he can warn the other hobos not to eat river fish?" Mike asked.

"Good thinking. Then afterwards, my brothers and I will take the old man up to the hospital, even if we have to rope him in the truck to get him there."

"So I go to school late?"

"Today you don't have to go to school at all, unless you want to," Pop said. "I got a special job for you. While we're at the hospital with the old man, I want you to grab his fishing pole and break it into a hundred pieces. Then throw the pieces into that filthy river and send them all the way to New Orleans. Your grandpap wants fish, we'll buy clean fish, at the market."

An hour later, Mike was riding up Penn Avenue alongside Pop. The pickle jar on the seat between them now contained a half-eaten catfish and a dead rat. Poor Old Sneaky, at least he wasn't in pain anymore.

As they passed St. Patrick's, Mike noticed a few kids arriving early. "Can we stop for a minute, Pop? Up at Eleventh Street. I need to talk to the guy who caught the fish."

Pop pulled the truck over at the corner of Penn and 11th Street and Mike watched out the window. After a few minutes, he saw Andy Simms hurrying toward school.

Mike hopped out of the truck and blocked the sidewalk so Simms had to stop.

"What are you doing here, Costa? This is my end of the street."

"I'll keep out of your way, just wanted to let you know. That fish you caught—looks like it was poisoned after all. We're taking it up to the hospital right now."

Simms nodded. "So I won't be eating any catfish for a while. All right, you said your piece. But this doesn't change anything, Costa. We're still enemies."

Mike didn't need a friend like Simms; he had Joseph. And wouldn't Joseph love to hear about all this over double chocolate malts at Klavon's? Mike could hardly wait until school let out so he could tell him. But he still had one thing left to say to Andy Simms.

"You're wrong, Simms. Finding out about the fish does change one thing. You still want to be my enemy, that's your business, but you won't be sick anymore."

"I ain't gonna say thanks, Macaroni Boy."

"Suit yourself," Mike shot back, turning toward the truck. Still, he couldn't help grinning. Macaroni Boy instead of Rat Boy, that was a start. And if only one side stayed enemies, did the battles have to go on? Mike had better things to do with his time.

"What are you smiling about, son?" Pop asked as he put the truck in gear and drove up Penn Avenue.

"Can't wait to tell Joseph," Mike said. "Now that we figured out about the catfish, we'll find the guys who blew up those bananas next. Just see if we don't."

Pop chuckled, then drove straight to the hospital, where he and Mike explained about the fish and the rat. Soon Grandpap was on his way to the hospital too with all the uncles keeping him from leaping out of the truck.

Mike stood alone along the chill gray water of the Allegheny River. Inch by inch he snapped off pieces of Grandpap's fishing pole and tossed them into the river, watching the bits of bamboo bobble and spin away downstream.

"Try chewing on some of this, you dumb old catfish," he called out. "You'll get splinters in your mouths and you deserve it."

At the thought of those nasty, whiskery fish chomping down on pieces of Grandpap's fishing pole, a big laugh rose from Mike's belly.

Yes, sir, he thought. *It's still the depression and all, but as of today, things are looking up. Grandpap's gonna start feeling better, so I got lots to laugh about.* And in his mind, he could see the sign he and Joseph would have some-day—COSTA AND RYAN, G-MEN. Or even better—COSTA AND RYAN, PRIVATE EYES.

Author's Note

THE central historical facts of this story are hunger and the Great Depression. Beginning in 1929 with the fall of the financial markets, the nation and then the world plunged into a period of brutal economic chaos. Banks closed; people lost their jobs, then their homes. Families went hungry and crops rotted in the fields for lack of buyers who could afford the food.

As time went by and the economy worsened, thousands of men called hobos rode in railroad boxcars and roamed the country in search of work. Entire families were uprooted, particularly in the Southwest, where a drought brought dust storms and destroyed miles and miles of cropland. Despair reigned through much of the 1930s, and the economic situation improved only slowly until World War

II broke out in Europe and American goods were again in demand by the countries at war.

In *Macaroni Boy*, Michael and Joseph's first hunch about the cause of sickness and death is right on target. The illness comes from the river, although indirectly.

For centuries, people living in cities and towns have drawn their drinking water from nearby rivers and streams. During the 1800s and early 1900s, scientists and doctors didn't know much about the effects of water pollution from sewage sources, so many rivers were filled with filthy, dangerous water. People who drank this water often got sick, and epidemics of cholera and typhoid were common.

In industrial cities such as Pittsburgh, mills and factories also dumped chemical wastes directly into the rivers. By the 1930s, although Pittsburgh still obtained drinking water from the Allegheny River, the drinking water was filtered and treated with chlorine to kill germs. But the river water itself was still a lethal soup.

Heavy metal is more than just a type of rock music. The term also refers to lead, mercury, arsenic, chromium and cadmium, which can be highly toxic to humans and animals. The unnamed culprit in this story is mercury, arsenic, or a combination of the two.

Mercury is a byproduct of metal manufacturing. Pittsburgh in the 1930s manufactured steel and aluminum, with some mills located beside the Allegheny River in the Strip District. Arsenic, another byproduct of industrial production, could have been dumped into the Allegheny from a leather tanning business on the north shore.

Both these chemicals can enter the food chain when fish are exposed to contaminated water. The metals build up in the fatty tissues of bottom-feeding fish such as catfish and carp. When a human (or a rat) eats such a fish, serious symptoms can result.

Concentration is one of the key factors in metal poisoning. In tiny amounts, such as the drink of river water the boys give Old Sneaky, the chemicals probably won't do much damage. But in larger doses, they become toxic, even lethal. In the story, Grandpap and Andy Simms both get sick from the poisoned catfish, but the rats, which have much smaller bodies, die.

Even today, with cleaner water and strict regulations about sewage treatment and industrial waste disposal, there are health advisories about eating only a small number of river-caught fish per month.

Metals can build up in human bodies too, not just in fish. In the story, Grandpap, Andy, the hobos and the rats suffer from *acute* metal poisoning, which means they have gotten sick from eating a large dose or two of contaminated fish. Their symptoms include upsets of the digestive system. Grandpap may also be suffering from *chronic,* or long-term, mercury poisoning (from eating lots of the fish over time), which can affect the central nervous system and might be contributing to his memory loss.

Another name for Grandpap's memory trouble is *dementia*. He forgets things and becomes confused easily, then grows angry when he realizes something is amiss. Dementia can have many causes, including strokes, Alzheimer's disease and improper doses of medications. It is always a difficult condition—for both the sufferer and the family.

Father Cox was a real person. An activist Catholic priest during the depression, he led an army of unemployed men—

Cox's Army—to Washington, D.C., in 1932 to protest the terrible economic conditions. His church, St. Patrick's, was the first Irish Catholic church built in Pittsburgh. During the 1930s Father Cox ran a soup kitchen and allowed unemployed, homeless men to build a shantytown on church property.

The banana explosion really happened too, on December 17, 1936. The banana warehouse still stands today at the corner of 22nd and Smallman Streets. Because I wanted the moonshiners to be part of this story, I changed the date so that it takes place before the repeal of Prohibition in December 1933.

Prohibition refers to the period from 1919 to 1933, when it was illegal to buy, sell or manufacture any sort of alcoholic beverage in the United States. Pittsburgh, with its three rivers, was a good place to transport illegal liquor during Prohibition, and various wooded areas on surrounding hillsides might have provided cover for moonshiners who cooked up corn whisky in homemade stills.

And Klavon's is real. Opened in 1920 as a drugstore with a soda fountain, it is now an ice cream parlor, still owned by the same family. If you visit Pittsburgh's Strip District, you can still rest your elbows on the dark green marble counter or spin on a Coca-Cola bottle cap seat while you wait for a chocolate milk shake or an Allegheny River float. On a hot day, you might find me there too.

Katherine Ayres, Pittsburgh

About the Author

KATHERINE AYRES says, "As a Pittsburgher, I'm surrounded by water. Two rivers, the Allegheny and the Monongahela, join together here to form the Ohio. Anytime I travel more than a mile or two from my house, I see a river flowing past or cross one on a bridge. And so the river became an important character in *Macaroni Boy*."

Writing is always a process of discovery for Ayres, who often looks to history for the people and places in her stories. Her most recent books for Delacorte Press are *Silver Dollar Girl* and *Stealing South: A Story of the Underground Railroad*. She also writes History Mysteries for Pleasant Company, and teaches writing at Chatham College, where she coordinates the Master of Arts program in children's and adolescents' writing.

When she is not writing or researching a book, she skis, golfs, gardens, and quilts. She and her husband have three grown children and one granddaughter.

You can visit Katherine Ayres on the web at:
www.chatham.edu/users/faculty/kayres